BAKER'S DOZEN

BAKER'S DOZEN

A MURPHY WESTERN

ETHAN J. WOLFE

FIVE STAR

A part of Gale, a Cengage Company

LIBRARY OF CONGRESS CATALOGING-IN-PUBLICATION DATA

Names: Wolfe, Ethan J., author.
Title: Baker's dozen : a Murphy western / Ethan J Wolfe.
Description: First edition. | Waterville, Maine : Five Star, [2020] | Series: The regulator series; book 6
Identifiers: LCCN 2019041846 | ISBN 9781432862206 (hardcover)
Subjects: GSAFD: Mystery fiction.
Classification: LCC PS3612.A5433 B35 2020 | DDC 813/.6—dc23
LC record available at https://lccn.loc.gov/2019041846

First Edition. First Printing: January 2021
Find us on Facebook—https://www.facebook.com/FiveStarCengage
Visit our website—http://www.gale.cengage.com/fivestar
Contact Five Star Publishing at FiveStar@cengage.com

Printed in Mexico
Print Number: 01   Print Year: 2021

For Michael Pare

For Michael Fine

PROLOGUE

Franklin Edson, the mayor of New York City, looked across his desk at Joseph Pulitzer, the newspaper mogul, and sighed loudly.

They were discussing the construction project for the pedestal that would house the Statue of Liberty, a gift to America from France.

"I know the fund-raising is lagging behind, Joseph, but what am I supposed to do? I can't exactly force the citizens to donate money, now can I?" Edson said. "They believe such expenditure is a waste of time and money, and frankly, so do I."

"My paper will print the name of every donor on the front page," Pulitzer said. "And I will pledge fifty-thousand dollars from my own pocket."

"The voters feel there is no need for such a statue, and I tend to agree with them," Edson said. "Especially with the opening of the Brooklyn Bridge being such a success and the other more important projects underway. The statue serves no real purpose other than as a glorified monument."

Pulitzer shook his head in a fury. "This statue will last a thousand years, Franklin," he said. "I will get the donors if I have to write about it every day in my papers."

"Good luck, Joseph," Edson said. "Right now, I have the police commissioner waiting in the hall, and we have pressing business."

"This isn't over, Franklin," Pulitzer said. "The pedestal will get built if it's the last thing I ever do."

After Pulitzer left Edson's office, Police Commissioner George Matsell was ushered in by Edson's secretary.

"Well?" Edson said as Matsell took a chair.

Matsell shook his head.

"How can someone murder six people in the span of two weeks and go undetected?" Edson asked.

"Seven, Mr. Mayor," Matsell said. "One last night. The same as the others."

"What are you doing about it?" Edson demanded.

"I have a dozen men searching the city for clues," Matsell said. "Unless you agree to allow me to go public with this, I can't even use the newspapers to ask for help from our citizens."

"Going public would cause a citywide panic clear to Brooklyn," Edson said. "Double your manpower immediately. I want this savage apprehended before he kills again."

"Yes, sir," Matsell said.

"Seven murdered in the streets," Edson said. "This is New York, not Tombstone. We are the most civilized city in the country. I have to leave for a meeting with Governor Cleveland in an hour," Edson said. "When I return tomorrow, I expect some progress to be made. Understood?"

Matsell nodded. "I understand, sir. Have a nice trip, Mr. Mayor."

"There is nothing nice about Albany," Edson said.

CHAPTER ONE

As they did every morning after breakfast, Murphy and Kai, his bride of two months, took a ride through the fields of his Tennessee farm.

Retired from the Secret Service after his last assignment, Murphy and Kai moved to the farm while they awaited construction on their second home in Fort Smith, Arkansas.

Kai was native to Fort Smith, having married a US marshal twenty years before. He died ten years ago when he was ambushed by the outlaws he was bringing to justice. She was part Navajo, Irish, and English. She spent many years among the Navajo and Sioux and spoke several different dialects of native languages, as well as Spanish and French.

Kai was taller than the average man of the day, muscular and slim and with piercing dark eyes and hair the color of coal.

Murphy loved her to the bone, even if he was too clumsy to speak of his love in words. In his lifetime, he had been many things. Farmer, soldier, and sniper during the war, a US Secret Service agent to President Grant, congressman, and finally back to the service.

He carried many scars, physically and mentally. The scars included the loss of his first wife and child to the war, the revenge upon the men who caused the loss, the memories of the war, and the death of the woman he would have married a few years ago, who was murdered.

All of it weighed heavily upon him, as if he walked around

carrying a sack of bricks on his back.

Kai had a way of healing his wounds and getting him to set the bag of bricks aside. She was funny and sarcastic and fearless and totally unafraid of him. She found it amusing how men seemed to be intimidated by Murphy, even if he was doing nothing except standing still.

Before she agreed to become his wife, Kai told Murphy, "I'm the one person you don't boss, Murphy. If you can live with that, we'll have a long and happy life together."

Murphy learned early on that trying to boss Kai was a lesson in futility, so he didn't even try.

They reached the south fields where hired hands were tending to cornstalks six feet high. When the corn was ready for harvest, it would be sent to Murphy's father's farm, about an hour's ride away, where Murphy's father used it to make bourbon whiskey.

Last year, Murphy's father produced four hundred barrels of the whiskey in his distillery. This year he had his sights on six hundred barrels, thanks to Murphy's added crop.

Murphy and Kai dismounted and walked to the edge of the hundred-acre crop.

"We need to return to Fort Smith soon," Kai said. "The house should be nearly complete in a month or so, and we have to contact the adoption agency in Little Rock for a progress report on our application."

"If the other fields are in as good a shape as this one, we can leave next week," Murphy said. "I'll tell the foreman to harvest and ship to my father's place and ready the fields for a quick turnaround."

The farm had four fields, of which two were always ready for harvest, while the other two were made ready for planting.

They returned to the horses. Murphy helped Kai into the saddle of the pinto he purchased for her as a wedding gift.

Murphy's massive horse, Boyle, towered over the pinto and, since the pinto arrived, they were inseparable.

"Race you home," Murphy said.

"Don't be silly," Kai said. "It's two steps for my horse to every one of your beast."

Murphy reached into his jacket pocket for his pipe and, as he did so, Kai yanked hard on the reins and the pinto raced forward.

"Well, hell, that's not fair," Murphy said.

In the kitchen of the farmhouse, after taking a roast out of the oven to cool, Kai looked out the window.

Murphy was beside the woodshed chopping wood. Shirtless, Murphy's upper body glistened from a sheen of sweat. With each blow of the ax, his heavy muscles rippled. He was the most heavily muscled man Kai had ever seen and was capable of great feats of strength, yet around her he was more boy than man, gentle as a kitten.

Kai opened the window. "The sun is down in fifteen minutes and supper is on the table," she said.

Murphy nodded. "Be right in," he said.

After dinner, Murphy boiled large pans of water and took them to the bathtub on the second floor. He had installed a drainage system using pipes to drain the tub into the ground. After dumping the boiling hot water into the tub, Murphy filled it with cold, using the secondary indoor pump.

"Kai, the bath is ready," Murphy said.

"Be right there."

Wearing a robe, Kai entered the large bathroom. She disrobed and delicately entered the tub, lowered herself, and waited for Murphy. The tub was large enough for two, and they often soaked together.

"We should hear from the adoption agency soon, I hope," Kai said.

"When they have something to tell us," Murphy said.

"It's taking too long," Kai said.

"I've heard stories of it taking years to get a child," Murphy said. "A few months is nothing to get concerned about."

The moment the words were out, Murphy knew they were the wrong ones to say. As a young woman living with the Navajo, Kai had suffered an internal injury that left her unable to have children.

Kai stared at Murphy. He tried to read her eyes. He saw a cross between crying and punching him in the nose.

"We can ride to town in the morning and send a telegram to the agency," he said.

"I don't want to pester them," Kai said.

"Sending a telegram isn't pestering," Murphy said.

Kai nodded. "All right," she said. "We'll send a telegram."

Nearly asleep, Murphy opened his eyes when Kai sighed heavily.

"What?" he said.

"Nothing. Go to sleep," Kai said.

Murphy closed his eyes again and started to drift off, and Kai sighed again.

"Okay, let's hear it," Murphy said.

"What?"

Murphy sat up, reached over to the nightstand, and felt for a wood match. He struck the match, lit the oil lamp on the stand, and set the flame to low.

"Whatever is causing you to sigh in the dark, that's what," he said.

Kai sat up beside him.

12

"Are you sorry you married a woman who can't give you children?"

"That came as no surprise to me, Kai," Murphy said. "I've known almost since the day we first met."

"But are you sorry?"

"Sorry is reserved for an apology, and I won't apologize for marrying a woman I love," Murphy said.

Kai shrugged. "Good answer," she said.

Murphy extinguished the lamp and settled in and closed his eyes. "Now can we get some sleep?" he said.

Kai nestled beside him. "Or," she said and whispered into his ear.

"Hell, I'd be a fool to say no," Murphy said.

CHAPTER TWO

Shirtless, Murphy helped his hands cut down the tall cornstalks and load them into wagons.

Not one for idle hands, dressed in dungaree pants with a blue cotton shirt, straw sun hat, and work gloves, Kai also carried stalks to the wagons.

The work went on for hours. At one point, after tossing stalks into a wagon, Kai paused to open a canteen and drink some water.

Something on the road far in the distance caught her eye. She set the canteen down and walked to Murphy's horse, Boyle. He fidgeted while she opened a saddlebag and reached inside.

"Stand still, you beast," Kai said as she removed binoculars from the saddlebag.

Kai used the binoculars to zoom in down the road, and then lowered the binoculars. "Damn that man," she said.

She replaced the binoculars into the saddlebag and discretely removed the Winchester rifle from Murphy's saddle sleeve.

She stood at the end of the wagon where Murphy couldn't see her and waited. Slowly, the horse-drawn carriage came into view until it finally arrived.

Kai aimed the Winchester rifle in the general direction of the carriage and said, "You can just turn around and go back where you came from, Mr. Burke."

William Burke, special assistant to President Chester Arthur, stepped down from the carriage and walked to Kai. "Put that silly thing away, Kai," he said. "I need to speak with your husband on an urgent matter."

"Yes. My husband," Kai said. "He belongs to me, not the president and certainly not to you."

Murphy left the field and walked to the wagon.

"I thought I heard your voice, William," Murphy said. "Kai, what are you doing with that rifle?"

"I was thinking of hunting varmint," Kai said.

"Murphy, we need to talk," Burke said.

"It's almost time for lunch. We might as well head to the house," Murphy said.

"Well, I'm not cooking for him," Kai said and slammed the Winchester back into the saddle sleeve.

Kai carried a tray that held three tall glasses of lemonade out to the front porch and set the tray on the round table in front of the chairs.

"Lunch will be ready in thirty minutes," she said and sat next to Murphy, glaring at Burke. "You might as well say what you came to say and be done with it."

Murphy picked up a glass and took a sip.

"Do you remember Mayor Franklin Edson of New York City?" Burke said.

Murphy nodded. "What about him?"

"There has been a string of very strange murders in New York that the police can't seem to get a handle on," Burke said.

"And that makes it our problem how?" Kai said.

"Kai, at least let Burke get it out," Murphy said.

"Only two months ago, you came home nearly dead from the last assignment," Kai said. "You didn't get out of bed for three days."

"It wasn't that bad," Murphy said.

Burke took a sip of lemonade and cleared his throat. "Seven

murders in a very quick time span," he said. "The police have no leads and no suspects. Edson asked Governor Cleveland for help, and Cleveland reached out to Arthur for use of the Secret Service. Frankly, the only member of the service with the—"

"Retired member," Kai said.

"Not officially," Burke said. "Arthur would like you to go to New York City and examine the evidence, what little there is, and assist the police with the investigation."

"People are murdered every day in this country. What is so special about New York City?" Kai said. "We were there just months ago. It smells like an outhouse in July."

"The entire country is tied into New York City," Burke said. "Right now, this scare has the stock market in shambles. As the stock market goes, so goes the economic health of the entire country."

Kai glared at Burke. "We haven't even had a proper honeymoon yet," she said.

"This shouldn't take too long, and Murphy will have help," Burke said.

"What kind of help?" Murphy asked.

"Pinkerton Agent Melvin Knoop," Burke said.

"Little Melvin? I though he decided to return to Scotland," Murphy said.

"Pinkerton convinced him to stay another year to work on a photograph-profiling system," Burke said.

"Just investigate the evidence?" Murphy said.

"Oh, damn it all," Kai said.

"That's all," Burke said.

"And Melvin assists me?" Murphy said.

"That's my understanding," Burke said.

Murphy looked at Kai.

"Don't look at me. I'm not returning to that outhouse," Kai said.

"I'm prepared to put you up in the best hotel in the city for as long as it takes," Burke said. "Plus expenses and salary.'

"Kai?" Murphy said.

"Can we see Julia and Grant?" Kai said, knowing she had been defeated.

"I expect so," Murphy said.

"I better see about lunch," Kai said.

"This is delicious. What is this?" Burke asked as he tasted the roasted birds Kai set on his plate.

"I went hunting before breakfast," Murphy said. "That's wild hen."

"My compliments, Kai," Burke said.

"I also brought back a sack of quail eggs for breakfast," Murphy said. "Kai makes omelets with them that are the best I've ever had."

"No need to butter me up, you two. I've already resigned myself to the idea we're returning to that cesspool you call a city," Kai said.

"It won't be for long, Kai," Burke said. "Once Murphy and Knoop get a handle on things, they will turn everything over to the city police."

"You said that about the kidnapped girl, and he came home a month later half dead with two bullets in him," Kai said. "When is enough enough? When he's in the ground?"

"This is a simple look at evidence and make a determination assignment," Burke said. "Think of it as part vacation for you."

"Vacation from what?" Kai stood up. "Who wants coffee?"

Seated in chairs on the porch, Burke looked at the majestic sunset on the horizon.

"Quite a view you have here," he said.

"Much better than those tall buildings in New York," Kai

said. "And it smells better here, too."

Murphy took a sip from his coffee cup, and then set the cup on the table in front of him. As he stuffed his pipe, he said, "Tell me about these strange murders, as you called them."

"All I can tell you is what I was told," Burke said. "Seven victims. All murdered seemingly at random with a .36 caliber lead ball. The New York City police have no suspects and no leads. The population is in a panic, and the stock market is headed into a downturn that could have a deep impact on the overall economy."

"A .36 caliber ball?" Murphy said. "Do they even still make them?"

"Doubtful, but there is probably a warehouse full of them somewhere, along with black powder and caps," Burke said.

Murphy nodded. "I assume you'll be making the trip to New York with us as a representative of Arthur?" he said.

"For a day or so," Burke said.

"When?" Kai asked.

"I'd like to leave in the morning," Burke said.

"We'll need to ride by my father's place so I can ask him to keep an eye on things," Murphy said.

Kai stood up. "Well, I'm glad I kept all those society clothes from Grant's book tour," she said. "And I guess I'll go and pack."

CHAPTER THREE

Kai and Burke sat in a private riding car and drank coffee. Outside the window, the scenery rolled by at fifty miles per hour.

Burke lit a cigar, puffed smoke, and sipped from his cup.

"We made plans to take our honeymoon in San Francisco as soon as the house in Fort Smith is finished," Kai said.

"This shouldn't interfere with that," Burke said. "I expect Murphy to be in New York no more than two weeks at most."

"You know how he gets when he's challenged," Kai said.

"I can't help how he gets, Kai," Burke said. "All he's needed for is to investigate the evidence and make a determination. If he gets how he gets, reel him in."

"Could you?"

"Not a chance in hell," Burke said. "But then, I'm not his wife."

Kai cocked an eyebrow at Burke. "Are you sure about that?"

The door to the riding car opened, and Murphy entered holding a fresh pot of coffee. "I made a reservation for lunch at one," he said.

Burke looked at his pocket watch.

Kai said, "That gives me time to freshen up," she said.

As he sliced into his plate of baked chicken, Murphy said, "Why do the police think the murders are random?"

"I expect that's a question they're hoping you and Knoop

will be able to answer," Burke said.

"When is he arriving?" Murphy asked.

"Tomorrow night," Burke said. "I figured that you and Kai and Knoop would be more comfortable in a townhouse rather than a hotel, so we rented one for you on the east side of the city."

"What time do we arrive?" Murphy asked.

"Sometime after breakfast. Around ten, I believe," Burke said.

"That gives us time to visit with Grant and Julia," Murphy said. "I'm sure he wouldn't mind seeing you again, Burke."

"I wouldn't bet on that," Burke said.

In their sleeping car, Murphy sat in a chair and watched Kai sleep. He had a small drink of his father's whiskey and smoked his pipe.

Seven random killings.

With a .36 caliber lead ball.

Who still used cap and ball after 1872?

Not many, for sure.

In the modern age of self-contained cartridges, the cap and ball was a thing of the past.

Maybe the killer was a really old man, who held onto the weapons he was used to as a young man.

Or.

Someone very knowledgeable about police sciences and knew modern weapons could be traced using serial numbers and that rifling made tracing an individual bullet to a specific weapon possible. That was a long shot though, as that kind of knowledge was still limited to but a few experts.

Or.

Kai rolled over and opened her eyes. "I thought the bed felt cold," she said. "What are you doing?"

"Just thinking," Murphy said.

"Can't you think in bed?"

Murphy tossed back the rest of his drink, left his pipe in the ashtray, and got into bed beside Kai.

"The lamp," Kai said.

Murphy extinguished the oil lamp on the table beside the bed.

"I don't want to sound ignorant on the subject, but exactly what is a townhouse?" Kai asked.

As a driver loaded their luggage into the rear storage compartment of his horse-drawn taxi, Kai looked around at the wide street known as Seventh Avenue. More people scurried about on the one block than lived in the entire town of Fort Smith.

Carriages and taxis were everywhere, and the streets were littered with horse dung. She noticed a man pushing a large barrel mounted on wheels. He used a shovel to scoop up the dung and place it in the barrel.

A policeman dressed in blue stood in the center of the street and directed traffic using, of all things, a whistle.

Murphy, anxious to get going, helped the driver with the luggage, assisted Kai into the carriage, and then sat beside her. Burke got in and sat to Murphy's right.

"Whenever you are ready, driver," Burke said.

The drive from the railroad station to the townhouse on East 23rd Street took close to an hour, as frequent stops were made at street crossings along the way, and traffic was heavy with carriages and cabs.

A lone rider on horseback was a thing of the past in modern-day Manhattan.

When the carriage arrived curbside at the townhouse, Kai looked up at the three-story, red-brick building and said, "How many people live here?"

"It will be you, Murphy, and Knoop, just the three of you," Burke said.

Murphy stepped down and helped Kai to the sidewalk. Burke followed and paid the driver.

"We need a carriage with a horse capable of taking the Murphys to Mount McGregor and back again by later this evening," Burke said. "Can you have a carriage ready in two hours?"

"I can, sir, but that is an expensive round-trip," the driver said.

"Of course it is," Burke said. "I'll expect a carriage in two hours."

"Very good, sir," the driver said as he removed the bags from the carriage and set them on the sidewalk.

"Come on, Murphy. I'll show you and Kai your home for the next two weeks," Burke said.

The first floor of the townhouse held the living room, parlor, kitchen, pantry, dining room, library, and den. The second floor was comprised of two bedrooms, two indoor water closets, a sewing room, and servants' quarters. The third floor was reserved for the master bedroom, two smaller bedrooms, another water closet, and a billiard room.

"Who lives in a house like this?" Kai asked.

"Wealthy Manhattan elite," Burke said.

"Do I have time to freshen up and change before we leave?" Kai asked.

Burke glanced at his pocket watch.

"We all do," he said.

After a two-hour ride north of Manhattan, the carriage arrived at the home of retired general and former President of the United States, Ulysses S. Grant. Before Murphy, Kai, and Burke stepped down from the carriage, the front door opened and Julia Grant stepped out to the porch.

"Hiram was so excited to receive your telegram," Julia said.

Kai raced up to the porch, where Julia greeted her with a warm hug and kiss on the cheek. Murphy was greeted in the same fashion, but all Burke got was a handshake.

"Hiram is in his study," Julia said. "And anxious to see you all."

Julia ushered them to the study where Grant sat behind a large, wood desk. He immediately stood and greeted Kai first with a kiss to the cheek.

"Even lovelier than the last time I saw you," he said.

"Kai, help me with the late lunch I prepared," Julia said. "Hiram, no whiskey."

The moment Julia and Kai left the room, Grant opened a desk drawer and produced a bottle of bourbon and three shot glasses.

He filled the three glasses and each man picked one up and tossed back the shot.

"Now that we got that out of the way, how are you, General?" Murphy asked.

"I survived our book tour, if that's what you mean," Grant said. "Hell, I survived the Mexican-American War in forty-six, the damned Civil War, and two terms as president, but I won't survive this damn throat cancer."

"Perhaps the doctors can . . ." Burke said.

"The doctors say I have less than two years," Grant said. "Why do you think I'm in such a damned hurry to finish my memoirs? I need to leave Julia well provided for after I'm gone."

Burke and Murphy exchanged glances.

"She will be, General," Murphy said. "You have our word on that."

"Our?" Grant said.

"Our," Burke said.

"How about another snort?" Grant said.

"General, Julia will skin us alive if she walked in and . . ." Murphy said.

"Julia knows to give me time for two drinks before she barges in and demands to know if I've been drinking," Grant said. "Now pour."

Murphy filled the three glasses. Each man lifted a glass and took a small sip.

"I assume old Burke here convinced you to check into those murders happening in New York," Grant said.

"More or less," Murphy said.

"Mostly more, I'm betting," Grant said.

There was a soft knock on the door. It opened and Kai poked her head in. "Lunch," she said.

After lunch, Grant, Murphy, and Burke sat in chairs on the front porch and drank black coffee laced with bourbon.

"Burke, when are you going to leave this man alone and let him enjoy life," Grant said. "God knows he's earned the right many times over."

"That isn't up to me, General," Burke said.

"That nincompoop occupying the White House made such a mess of the last detail, it damned near cost Murphy his life," Grant said.

"Murphy could always refuse an assignment," Burke said.

Murphy lit his pipe and sipped coffee.

"General, when will your memoirs be published?" Murphy said.

"Soon," Grant said. "Hopefully, I'll still be around to cash the check and set up things properly for Julia."

"I know you will be, General," Burke said.

Grant looked at Murphy. "How about you, Murphy? If you get your fool head blown off on one of these assignments, is your widow properly taken care of?"

Before Murphy could answer, the porch door opened and Julia and Kai stepped out.

"Hiram, it's a long drive back to Manhattan," Julia said.

"I suppose it is," Grant said.

"I've invited Kai to come stay with us while Murphy is working, if she gets bored with Manhattan," Julia said.

"That's a fine idea," Grant said.

"I'm going to change and get comfortable," Kai said when they arrived at the townhouse.

"Burke and I will wait for Knoop in the living room," Murphy said.

Murphy and Burke removed their jackets and hung them on the coatrack. In the living room, Murphy poured two drinks of bourbon and gave one to Burke.

They took seats in comfortable leather chairs. Murphy lit his pipe. Burke lit a cigar.

"Grant is right, you know," Murphy said. "If I go tomorrow, Kai isn't prepared. I need a good lawyer to work things out for me."

"There are several right here in New York I know personally," Burke said. "Including the man who set up Grant's estate."

"Can you . . . ?"

"I will."

"Without . . ."

"I won't say a word to Kai."

"I hear a carriage," Murphy said.

"Knoop must be early."

Burke and Murphy went to the door, opened it, and looked down the steps to the sidewalk where a carriage driver was unloading two large suitcases. After the driver left, Knoop started to drag the suitcases to the front steps.

Knoop, a short man shaped like a pear, was dressed in a suit of clothes best suited for a carnival barker. He was struggling hard with his luggage.

"Help him before he passes out," Burke said.

Murphy went down the steps and said, "I got them, Melvin."

"Mr. Murphy, you startled me," Knoop said.

"Go on up," Murphy said, as he picked up the suitcases and followed Knoop up the steps.

"Mr. Burke," Knoop said.

"Hello, Melvin," Burke said.

"Is that Melvin?" Kai said from inside the house.

Knoop rushed past Burke to where Kai stood in the living room. "Kai, I'm so happy to see you," he said.

Kai hugged Knoop and kissed him on the cheek.

"Late supper," Kai said. She looked at Murphy as he entered the living room. "Be a dear and take Melvin's bags to his room."

Kai and Knoop linked arms, and she took him to the kitchen.

Murphy looked at Burke.

"You heard her. Take his bags to his room," Burke said.

"I'm going to try that indoor bathtub," Kai said after dinner. "Murphy, don't be too late coming to bed."

Murphy, Burke, and Knoop moved from the dining room to the living room, where Murphy filled three shot glasses with his father's bourbon.

Burke lit a cigar.

Murphy lit his pipe. Knoop coughed.

"So I hear you've been working on a photograph system at Pinkerton's," Murphy said.

"Putting together a photo book of all known criminals in Chicago for the police to use for identification purposes," Knoop said. "Mr. Pinkerton plans to take it to Washington to use on a federal level."

"Sounds exciting," Burke said.

"Hardly, but much of police work is tedious and routine," Knoop said. "Which is why I jumped at the chance to come to New York and work with Mr. Murphy again."

Burke sipped bourbon, puffed on his cigar, and said, "I know that Murphy feels the same."

Knoop grinned proudly. "We did make a good team last time, didn't we?"

"Marvelous," Murphy said.

Knoop sipped his bourbon and coughed several times.

"What information do you have on these murders, Melvin?" Murphy asked.

"Not much, I'm afraid," Knoop said. "Just that seven murders seem to have been committed at random with a .36 caliber ball. I was asked to join you to study evidence and make determinations."

Murphy finished his drink and then stood up. "Get some sleep, Melvin. We'll have a long day tomorrow, I'm sure."

After Murphy left the living room, Knoop turned to Burke. "Mr. Burke, did you ever find out Mr. Murphy's first name?"

"No, Melvin, I surely didn't," Burke said. "And take my advice. Don't pester him about it."

CHAPTER FOUR

Mayor Franklin Edson and Police Commissioner George Matsell were waiting for Murphy, Knoop, and Burke in the conference room at City Hall. A spread of fresh pastry, coffee, tea, and juice lay on a serving cart beside the table.

"Mr. Murphy, the City of New York thanks you for your assistance in this terrible crime, and also to you, Mr. Knoop," Edson said. "Mr. Burke, please thank the president for me for the use of his Secret Service."

"I will," Burke said.

Once everyone was seated, a chef's aide entered the room and served coffee and pastry to each person at the table, then left.

"Mr. Murphy, Mr. Knoop, the situation, such as it is, well, the stock market is not reacting favorably, as you can imagine," Edson said. "Neither is the general public in the city, as you can also imagine. Commodities such as beef, corn, and wheat are slumping, and it could cause a recession in the country, even a depression, as it were."

Murphy sighed. Burke glanced at Murphy and, knowing the limits of Murphy's patience, said, "Rest assured, Mr. Mayor, that Murphy and Mr. Knoop will do everything possible to assist the city police to apprehend this murderer."

"I'd like to get started as soon as possible," Murphy said.

"Understandable," Edson said. "I have a meeting with the city council in a few minutes, so I will turn this meeting over to

28

Commissioner Matsell."

With a slight head bow, Edson stood and left the room.

Knoop grabbed a donut, dunked it in his coffee, and bit off a piece.

"Shall we get started?" Murphy said.

"We can walk to my office at police headquarters," Matsell said. "I have stored all evidence in my office, as this is a top priority to the city."

"I'll leave you as well," Burke said. "Murphy, Melvin, I'll see you both back at the townhouse."

Kai was in the parlor when Burke returned to the townhouse.

"Mr. Burke, I'm glad you are here," Kai said. "It's not even noon, and I am about to go loco from boredom."

"Why don't we go to lunch?" Burke suggested. "The city's oldest restaurant tavern is just a few blocks' walk from here."

"Give me a few minutes to change," Kai said.

Murphy looked at the map of Manhattan resting on a table in Matsell's office. The seven murders were each marked by a red *X*. A sheet of paper, typed, lay beside the map, listing the names of the victims.

The first victim was John O'Connor, age listed as sixty-three. He was found shot dead one city block from his residence on West 4th Street at nine p.m. on a Wednesday.

Victim number two was Joseph Garrison, age listed as sixty-four, and he was killed two blocks from his residence on West 14th Street. He was found at nine-twenty p.m. on a Monday.

Jefferson Tyler, victim number three, age listed as sixty-seven, was killed in front of the building he lived in on West 35th Street at eight-forty p.m. on a Thursday.

Victim number four, Wilford Porter, age sixty-three, was killed one city block from his apartment on West 147th Street at ten p.m. on a Friday.

The fifth victim, Andrew O'Keefe, age seventy-one, was killed walking his dog in Riverside Park one block from his residence on West 19th Street at eight thirty-five p.m. on a Sunday.

Francis Finnegan, age sixty-one, the sixth victim, was killed in front of his apartment building on West 10th Street at nine forty-five p.m. on a Saturday.

The seventh victim, Dennis Miles, age sixty-two, was killed one block from his building on East 71st Street at six-fifteen a.m. on a Monday.

"Commissioner, who interviewed the families of the victims?" Murphy asked.

"The first two were interviewed by my detectives," Matsell said. "The next five by my captains in the detective squad."

"And what were their findings?" Murphy said.

In the background, Knoop pulled a donut from a pocket and nibbled on it.

"Solid family men, fathers and grandfathers," Matsell said. "Retired, most of them, and living on modest pensions and savings. No known enemies to speak of, and their families could think of no one who would want to murder the victims."

"Men don't always tell their families their secrets," Murphy said.

Knoop stood next to Murphy and looked at the map on the table.

"What are you suggesting, Mr. Murphy? That each man shared a common secret that got them all killed?" Matsell said.

"That had to have occurred to you," Murphy said.

"It has, but what does it mean?" Matsell said. "My detectives tell me the men weren't related and didn't know one another."

"All Irish, English, and Scottish names," Knoop said. "That's a common thread."

"Are you saying these men were killed simply because they

are British in origin?" Matsell said. "Because if you are, the killer will target half of Manhattan."

"I'm not saying that at all, but just stating that their race is a common thread," Knoop said.

"Commissioner, we'd like all reports and evidence you have gathered up to this point," Murphy said. "And I'd like to see the bullets."

"The bullets?" Matsell said.

"Do you have them?" Murphy asked.

"My desk."

Matsell went to his desk, sat, and opened a drawer. He removed a stack of files and a jar containing eleven lead balls.

Murphy picked up the jar and looked at the lead balls. They were damaged on impact, but recognizable as .36 caliber balls.

"Commissioner, we will take these reports, study them overnight, and report back to you tomorrow morning," Murphy said. "And tell me: where is the police pistol range?"

"Indoor or out?" Matsell said.

"Out."

"Eleventh Avenue and 31st Street."

"I'd like to visit it tomorrow," Murphy said. "After we report to you in the morning."

"I'll arrange it," Matsell said. "Do you wish a carriage home?"

"It's a short walk," Murphy said. "And Melvin can use the exercise."

As Murphy and Knoop walked east to the townhouse, Knoop, gasping, said, "Mr. Murphy, wait. I need you to slow down a bit. I have to take two steps to your one."

"Sorry, Melvin," Murphy said and slowed his pace.

Knoop got into step beside Murphy. "There are many questions we didn't ask that should have been asked," he said.

"Such as?"

"Six of the seven victims were killed after dark and one before sunrise," Knoop said. "It suggests the killer knew their habits and patterns."

"It does, doesn't it?" Murphy said. "And?"

"And . . . if the killer knew their habits and patterns, it means he took the time to study his victims, which means the murders aren't random."

Holding the files under his right arm, Murphy looked at Knoop. "Underestimate Melvin Knoop at your own peril," he said.

Knoop looked up at Murphy and grinned.

"Burke is leaving for Washington in the morning. I suggest we take him to dinner tonight," Murphy said.

Murphy, Knoop, and Burke gathered in the study to read the police reports.

Murphy and Knoop took extensive notes.

Burke, smoking a cigar, said, "I agree with your assessment that these murders aren't random. Whoever shot those men knew where they would be and when."

"The interviewing detectives and Matsell's reports state that the wives and surviving family members have no idea who would want the victims dead," Murphy said. "They also claim their husbands didn't know the other victims."

"After the third murder, they went back and asked family members if they knew the next victim," Knoop said. "They claim they don't."

"There are almost two million people in New York City, so I'm not surprised," Burke said. "In Washington, I barely know my neighbors, and I can spit to their houses from my front porch. Washington is a fraction of New York's size."

Kai opened the door to the study. "I'm ready," she said.

★ ★ ★ ★ ★

The carriage ride to Delmonico's Restaurant on Fifth Avenue and 26th Street took about twenty minutes. The carriage seated four, with Murphy and Kai facing Burke and Knoop. Traffic was not nearly as congested as earlier in the day, and the air was cooler and fresher.

Since it opened in 1837, Delmonico's had been one of the premier restaurants in Manhattan. On any given night, long lines were expected and tolerated.

Since management of Delmonico's was familiar with Burke and his VIP status, they were ushered to a private room reserved for their elite clientele.

Steaks were ordered all the way around, and Burke requested a bottle of their best wine.

"How long do you think this will take?" Burke asked. "I'd like to put Arthur's mind at ease."

"Nothing will put his mind at ease except winning reelection," Murphy said. "God forbid," he added.

Burke looked at Kai.

"You asked for him, not me," Kai said. "I was happy to stay home and harvest cornstalks."

"Throw me a bone, Murphy. Something I can tell Arthur," Burke said.

"You can tell Arthur he can go—" Murphy said and stopped when Kai kicked him under the table.

"I can tell Arthur what?" Burke said.

"That Melvin and I will dedicate ourselves to helping the police find and apprehend this murderer with utmost diligence," Murphy said.

Kai looked at Murphy. "See? You actually can speak in full sentences when you put your mind to it," she said.

Burke looked away and grinned.

The waiter arrived with a trolley and served dinner.

"Kai, you would be a refreshing welcome to the stuffed shirts on the Hill if Murphy were inclined to return to politics," Burke said.

"Would they be so welcoming if they knew I'm part Navajo?" Kai asked. "That I lived with the Sioux and speak their language?"

"I can remember a time not so long ago when the Irish were looked upon with less than favorable intentions," Burke said. "The Civil War ended less than twenty years ago, and the people elected the first black man to Congress just three years after the surrender. Times change, Kai, and so do people."

"Times don't change that much and not overnight," Kai said. "The Navajo tribe will live on a reservation for—"

"The dates of the murders and days of the week indicate that the murderer has observed his victims for quite some time and knows their habits very well," Knoop said. "So it stands to reason that this kind of planning requires high intelligence and a lot of patience."

"Ah, there you are. Melvin," Murphy said.

"Sorry. I was just thinking out loud," Knoop said.

"Think quietly, so I can enjoy my steak," Burke said.

"What you said at dinner is absolutely correct," Murphy said to Knoop.

Murphy, Burke, and Knoop were having a drink in the study after returning home from Delmonico's.

"This killer is no ordinary Wild West shooter," Murphy said. "He has a plan and, so far, has executed it flawlessly and avoided detection."

"Do you think he will kill again?" Burke asked.

Murphy looked at Knoop.

"Count on it," Knoop said.

Burke tossed back his drink and reached for the bottle and

filled his shot glass. "I think I'll take this one to my room," he said.

After Burke left, Murphy said, "Robbery isn't a motive. The reports state that their wallets and valuables were still intact. Tomorrow, I'd like to see the medical examiner's report. Right now, I'm joining my wife."

"Mr. Murphy, why .36 caliber balls?" Knoop said. "Why not regular bullets? Do you think our killer actually knows about ballistics and modern forensics?"

"Anything is possible, Melvin," Murphy said. "Good night."

Murphy thought Kai was asleep when he quietly got into bed, but she rolled over in the dark and said, "If you even think about running for Congress again, I will show you the Navajo in me, and it won't be pretty."

"Who said I . . ." Murphy said.

"Sometimes I think you'd rather be married to Burke," Kai said and rolled over and gave Murphy her back.

"I never said anything about—" Murphy said.

"And don't," Kai said. "And don't even think it. Now be quiet. I'm tired and want to sleep."

Murphy sighed softly and closed his eyes.

After several minutes passed, Kai rolled over again and said, "Well?"

Murphy opened his eyes. "Well what?"

"Are you or aren't you?"

"Aren't I what?" Murphy said.

"Never mind," Kai said. "Go play with Melvin and find your killer."

"Play with—"

Kai moved again and sat on top of Murphy. "I'm awake now, thanks to you," she said. "So you might as well do something about it."

As Kai kissed him, Murphy thought, *every last one of them is crazy.*

CHAPTER FIVE

"It had to occur to you that these murders aren't random," Murphy said. "That there is some purpose driving the killer we are unaware of yet."

"It has, but the victims are completely unlinked," Matsell said.

"From our point of view," Murphy said.

"All seven murders were committed after dark or before sunrise," Knoop said. "The killer studied his victims and learned their habits to avoid detection. That tells us he has a specific purpose in mind, and that makes these calculated acts and not random ones."

"Driver, the next block," Matsell said.

They were in Matsell's personal carriage, a luxury provided by the city. Murphy held a wood box on his lap.

"Where are the victims' clothing and personal belongings?" Murphy asked.

"Evidence warehouse a block from the range," Matsell said.

"We'll go there after we visit the range," Murphy said.

At the range, Murphy set the wood box on a shooting table and opened it. Inside was an 1851 Navy Colt revolver, caps, .36 caliber balls, and a small horn of black powder.

"I carried the Navy Colt throughout the war and right up until 1870, when Colt sold conversion kits for the new self-contained cartridge," Murphy said. "I haven't had the need to fire it in ten or more years."

He lifted the Colt and checked the action several times and then handed it to Knoop.

"One of the finest weapons ever made," Murphy said and took the Colt back from Knoop. "Wild Bill Hickok carried a set right up until the day he died."

Murphy took the horn and loaded powder into each chamber. Then he carefully placed one lead ball into the chambers and tamped each one down with the loading lever.

"In 1865, Hickok killed a man in a duel, shooting him through the heart at a distance of seventy-six feet," Murphy said.

Murphy stuck a cap onto the six nipples.

"The problem is that it takes so long to reload," he said. "Which is why Hickok always carried two Navy Colts."

"I've seen pictures of Hickok," Knoop said.

Murphy turned to Matsell. "Ask the instructor to bring the target back to fifty feet."

Matsell motioned and the instructor cranked a handle and the target, suspended on a thin rope, moved back to fifty feet.

"Step back, Melvin," Murphy said.

Knoop moved back and to the side.

Murphy cocked the Navy Colt at his side and then brought it up and fired without aiming. Then, in quick succession, he fired the remaining five shots.

"Bring it in while I reload," Murphy said.

Matsell motioned, and the instructor reeled in the target. Murphy had put all six shots into the center ring of the bull's-eye.

"Next target at maximum," Murphy said.

"That's one hundred feet," Matsell said.

Murphy nodded as he reloaded the Navy Colt. The instructor set the target at one hundred feet and Murphy licked his finger and felt the wind.

"Slight breeze off the river," he said.

Murphy cocked, aimed, and fired six times.

The instructor reeled in the target and again all six shots were in the center ring in the bulls-eye.

"You can handle a gun," Matsell said. "My compliments, Mr. Murphy."

"Want to give it a try, Melvin?" Murphy said.

"I couldn't hit a buffalo standing in front of me," Knoop said.

"All right then, let's move on to the evidence warehouse," Murphy said.

"What are you looking for?" Matsell asked. "My detectives have already been over the evidence and found nothing of any use."

Murphy and Knoop had set seven boxes on a long table in the evidence warehouse.

"Melvin, do you see any powder burns on any of the victims' clothing?" Murphy asked.

"I do not," Knoop said.

"Make a note in your notebook."

Knoop scribbled a note in his pad.

Murphy looked at Matsell. "So the shooter wasn't at close range when he shot his victims," Murphy said. "As you saw, the Navy Colt is extremely accurate up to one hundred feet. How wide is the widest street in Manhattan?"

"Around sixty feet," Matsell said.

"So the shooter didn't need to be close to his victims to kill them," Knoop said.

"Assuming he's as good a shot as Mr. Murphy," Matsell said.

"Obviously he is," Knoop said. "Or the victims wouldn't be dead."

"Is anything missing from their personal belongings?" Murphy asked.

"Everything that was found on the bodies is listed into evidence and in each crate," Matsell said.

"So we can cross off robbery as a motive," Murphy said. "And move on to the clothing."

"You already said there were no powder burns," Matsell said.

"Melvin, make a list of the labels on the jackets, pants, and shirts," Murphy said. "Maybe they shop at the same stores and have the same tailor."

"When your detectives and you spoke to the families of the victims, did you discuss finances?" Murphy said.

"Finances?" Matsell said. "They just lost their husbands and fathers. I figured to wait until the right time to—"

"Now is the right time," Murphy said. "Melvin, we can see at least three families today and the rest tomorrow."

"I'll accompany you," Matsell said.

"That's not necessary, Commissioner," Murphy said. "You must have a hundred other things that need your attention."

"None others that have the mayor breathing down my neck," Matsell said.

"Melvin, are you finished with the list?" Murphy said.

"Yes."

"Which family is closest?" Murphy said.

The widow of Jefferson Tyler opened the apartment door and looked at Matsell.

"I'm terribly sorry to disturb your time of grief, but we have some questions that are important to our investigation," Matsell said.

"I've already answered all of your questions, what is possibly left to ask?" Mrs. Tyler said.

"This is Mr. Murphy and Mr. Knoop," Matsell said. "They

are investigators retained by the city to assist in the investigation and in finding the murderer of your husband. This won't take long."

Mrs. Tyler looked up at Murphy and then down at Knoop. "I'll put on some tea," she said.

Five minutes later, Mrs. Tyler served tea in the kitchen.

"My husband was very fond of tea," she said. "His grandparents came over from England just before the start of the Revolutionary War and fought on the side of the colonies."

Knoop sampled the tea. "Earl Grey," he said.

"You know your tea, Mr. Knoop," Mrs. Tyler said.

"Mrs. Tyler, where did your husband buy his clothing?" Murphy asked.

"His clothing?" Mrs. Tyler said. "I'm afraid he hadn't purchased anything new since he retired from his job three years ago. He worked for the city, you know. He was an auditor in the budgets department."

"I read that he had a pension and savings account," Murphy said.

"Yes. We were getting by just fine," Mrs. Tyler said. "What does this have to do with the man who shot him?"

"We're trying to establish a pattern of the man who killed your husband and the other six men," Murphy said. "Is it possible your husband owed money you didn't know about?"

"The police already asked that question. I didn't know the answer then and I don't now. If he owed money, no one has contacted me about it."

"I know you were asked if your husband knew any of the other six men who were killed, and you said you didn't believe so," Murphy said. "But how could you be sure? Maybe some of them purchased clothing at the same tailor or used the same barber?"

Mrs. Tyler sipped some tea as she thought for a moment.

"He purchased most of his clothing at Roth's Tailor Shop on Broadway and Houston Street. His barber was just a few blocks from here. Feldman's Barber Shop."

"The police report stated your husband was returning from his nightly walk after dinner when he was shot," Murphy said. "Did he walk every night?"

"Every morning after breakfast and every night after dinner," Mrs. Tyler said. "My husband was very spry. Before he retired, he would often walk to work and home, a distance of thirty blocks each way."

"Did you ever accompany him on his walks?" Murphy asked.

"In the morning. After dinner, I had to clean the dirty crockery, and I was usually too tired by then."

"What time did he usually walk at night?" Murphy asked.

"Seven-thirty, usually. He'd walk for about an hour or so."

"Alone?"

"At night, when I didn't go with him, yes. Alone."

"And where did he go?"

"Anywhere. Uptown, downtown, the park. It didn't matter to him. He loved the city, and he loved to walk."

Murphy looked at Knoop. "Melvin, any questions for Mrs. Tyler?"

"Where can I buy some of this tea?" Knoop asked.

"What do you think, Melvin?" Murphy said.

"I wouldn't rule out the possibility that some of Mr. Tyler's nightly walks included a walk to a mistress," Knoop said.

"You're joking," Matsell said.

They were walking to Feldman's Barber Shop on West 32nd Street.

"Tyler wouldn't be the first married man with a mistress," Murphy said.

"What did you . . . I mean, what leads you to think he was

visiting a mistress the night he was killed?" Matsell asked.

"There is a faint aroma of perfume on his suit jacket," Knoop said. "And a few strands of long blond hair. Mrs. Tyler is brown speckled with gray."

"I see," Matsell said. "Apparently my people missed that point."

"It's doubtful Tyler was killed by a mistress," Murphy said.

They reached the barbershop. A man of about sixty was finishing a haircut, and they waited for the customer to leave before entering the shop.

"Are you Mr. Feldman?" Matsell asked.

"I am, and I think you gentlemen aren't here for a haircut," Feldman said.

"Mr. Feldman, do you know Jefferson Tyler?" Murphy asked.

"Of course. Twenty years or more I cut his hair," Feldman said.

"You are aware of the other six men who were murdered recently?" Murphy said.

"Who isn't in this city?"

"Were any of them your customers?" Murphy said.

"Mister, I do thirty or more cuts a day. Do you really expect me to remember all of them?" Feldman said.

Knoop opened the briefcase he was carrying and showed photographs of the other six victims to Feldman.

Feldman looked at each photograph carefully and then shook his head. "None of these men were my customers," he said.

On the ride south to Roth's Tailor Shop, Knoop said, "Can we stop for lunch?"

"Please don't put the idea of running for Congress in his head, Burke," Kai said. "You know how stubborn Murphy can be when an idea takes root in his mind, especially if he feels challenged."

"I was joking about that," Burke said.

"Murphy considers you and Grant his closest friends," Kai said. "He takes what you tell him seriously."

They were in the parlor having coffee, while Burke waited for his taxi to arrive.

"Kai, if ever there was a man who knows his own mind, it's the one you married," Burke said.

"I know that," Kai said. "I've also watched him chop at a thick stump with an ax for weeks on end when he could have hitched a team of plow horses to do the job in a matter of minutes. When he gets an idea to do something, he does it, no matter what. We're building a second home in Fort Smith and are waiting for a child from an adoption agency. Don't plant the seed of running for Congress again."

"You don't have anything to worry about, Kai," Burke said. "Even a blind man can see how devoted to you Murphy is."

There was a knock on the front door. "Taxi for Mr. Burke," the driver said.

"Murphy and Knoop will wrap this up in a few days and then you'll be home, so stop worrying and enjoy your time in New York," Burke said.

After Burke left, Kai sat in the parlor with a cup of coffee.

"Enjoy New York," she said aloud. "I'd sooner enjoy living in an outhouse."

"Mr. Tyler purchased two suits a year while he was working," Roth said. "He also would purchase six white shirts and a dozen ties every year, as well. Since he retired, I can't say that I've seen him but once or twice."

"What about the other murder victims? Are they customers of yours?" Murphy asked.

"No," Roth said. "I know every customer of mine by first and last name and by sight. If any of the other men killed by that madman were my customers, I would recognize the name."

Back in Matsell's carriage, Matsell said, "Where to next?"

"We have time to speak with one more family," Murphy said. "Melvin, which is closest?"

Knoop looked at his notes. "Joseph Garrison on West 14th Street."

"I'm Mrs. Garrison, who are you?" Mrs. Garrison said when she opened the door to her townhouse apartment.

"Police Commissioner Matsell. This is Special Agent Murphy and his associate, Melvin Knoop. They are assisting me with the investigation into your husband's murder."

"Come in. I'll put on some fresh coffee."

A few minutes later, Mrs. Garrison served coffee at the kitchen table.

"Mrs. Garrison, I've read all the police reports," Murphy said. "I know that on the evening your husband was killed, he was returning from a card game at a friend's house. You said that he played cards with his friends every Monday night from six to nine and then walked home."

"Yes," Mrs. Garrison said.

"We have his friends' names, and they were all interviewed by the police," Murphy said. "His place of business before he retired and everything else, you gave the police. Since then, is there anything else you thought of that you'd like to share?"

"I wish there was," Mrs. Garrison said. "My husband had many friends and no enemies I'm aware of. Whoever did this had a reason, but for the life of me, I can't think of what it is."

Murphy and Knoop opted to walk back to the townhouse from the Garrison apartment.

"We'll talk to the other widows in the morning," Murphy said.

"The lack of evidence is frustrating," Knoop said.

"People don't shoot people without a reason," Murphy said. "Even if the reason borders on the insane, there is a reason. We need to keep poking and prodding until we uncover some reason and hope it leads us to the killer."

"I'm hungry," Knoop said.

"Of course you are," Murphy said.

"This is wonderful," Knoop said as he sliced into a Cornish hen.

"I went for a walk today and found a large market at Union Square," Kai said.

Murphy looked at Kai. She smiled at him.

"I saw many fine private schools on my walk," Kai said. "A child could get an excellent education in a private school."

"I went to private school in Scotland," Knoop said.

Murphy looked at Knoop as Knoop forked a hunk of hen into his mouth.

"Tomorrow while you boys are out chasing rainbows, I'm—" Kai said.

"Chasing rainbows?" Murphy said.

"Tomorrow, I will visit some of the museums and art galleries I read about in the guide book," Kai said.

"I'd like to see them myself," Knoop said.

"Why don't you accompany me?" Kai said.

"Melvin has work to—" Murphy said.

"Maybe I was rash in my criticism of New York," Kai said. "People don't seem to notice or care that I'm part Navajo. This may not be a bad place to raise a child."

"Kai, before you start talking about—" Murphy said.

"Melvin, would you like another hen?" Kai said.

"I would, thank you," Knoop said.

Kai stood and walked to the door of the dining room, paused, and looked back at Knoop. "Save room for dessert. I made apple pie with fresh apples I got at the market."

"Kai is a wonderful woman," Knoop said.

Murphy looked at Knoop. "Kai, my little friend, wants something."

"What is it? What do you want?" Murphy said as he entered the bedroom.

Kai sat at the dressing table, wrapped in a white robe and brushing her long, dark hair.

"Who said I wanted anything?" she said.

"The little voice in my head."

Kai stroked her hair and then set the brush aside and stood.

"Well?" Murphy said.

Kai turned down the bed, lowered the flame. and looked at Murphy. "Well what?"

"What is it you want?" Murphy said.

Kai opened the robe; it fell away and Murphy looked at her naked body.

"I fell for that 'moment of weakness is the best time to get your man to do something' once, Kai," Murphy said.

Kai got into bed. "Suit yourself," she said. "Turn off the lamp when you come to bed."

"Oh, hell," Murphy said.

Kai nestled her face into Murphy's chest and said, "Are you feeling weak?"

"Whatever it is you want, ask," Murphy said.

"I'd like to spend some time with the Grants," Kai said. "I can't stand this city."

"You said you saw many fine—"

"Never mind what I said before," Kai said. "Mind what I'm saying now."

"I suppose I can wire Grant in the morning," Murphy said.

"I already sent him a telegram when I went out," Kai said. "Grant is sending a carriage for me in the morning."

"Then why did you—?" Murphy said with frustration in his voice.

"Be quiet," Kai said and rolled on top of Murphy. "And I'll make your knees buckle."

Crazy. They're all crazy, Murphy thought.

CHAPTER SIX

Murphy loaded Kai's luggage into the carriage and then waited for Kai to emerge from the townhouse.

Kai came out holding Knoop's right hand.

"Make sure you keep his Irish temper in check, Melvin," Kai said. "You know how he can get."

"I'll do my best," Knoop said.

"Oh for . . ." Murphy said.

Kai released Knoop's hand and looked up at Murphy. "Behave yourself," she said and kissed him.

Murphy boosted Kai into the carriage, and Kai waved as the driver pulled away from the curb.

Murphy looked at Knoop, who was wiping a tear from his eye.

"Marvelous," Murphy said. "Come on, Melvin. Let's go to work."

Murphy and Knoop examined their notes in the study while they waited for Matsell's carriage to arrive.

"Who should we see today, Melvin?" Murphy asked.

"We worked Lower Manhattan yesterday. Let's try Upper today," Knoop said.

"Miles, Porter, and O'Keefe," Murphy said.

"We can work the remaining Lower Manhattan tomorrow," Knoop said.

"Miles is closest," Murphy said. "We'll work our way north."

"I think I hear a carriage," Knoop said.

The widow of Dennis Miles opened the door to the large and lavish apartment on East 71st Street and said, "Commissioner Matsell, have you some news?"

"I'm afraid I bring questions," Matsell said. "This is Special Agent Murphy and Mr. Knoop and they are assisting me with the investigation. May we come in and talk for a few minutes?"

"I'll make some coffee," Mrs. Miles said.

A few minutes later, Mrs. Miles served coffee and almond cookies at the kitchen table.

"Almond cookies were my husband's favorite," Mrs. Miles said.

Knoop scooped up a cookie and popped it into his mouth.

"Mrs. Miles, I've read all the police reports regarding your husband and I just have a few questions," Murphy said. "He was an early riser and walked for thirty minutes every morning before breakfast, is that correct?"

"We were married thirty-six years, and the only times he didn't walk before breakfast were if it was snowing or raining so hard, walking would be dangerous," Mrs. Miles said. "Otherwise, you could set your watch by him."

"I've read all the statements from family, friends, his business associates, and all concur that your husband was very well liked and respected," Murphy said.

"Yes, very much so," Mrs. Miles said.

"Is there anything you can tell us that you might have thought of since the last time you spoke to the police?" Murphy said.

Mrs. Miles looked at Knoop, who was eating another cookie. "No. Wait. Yes. I did remember my husband saying that the name Francis Finnegan sounded very familiar to him when he read it in the newspapers."

"Familiar how?" Murphy asked.

"I don't know, and neither did he," Mrs. Miles said. "He just said he remembered the name Finnegan from somewhere, but he couldn't remember where. Two weeks later, he was dead."

"In your husband's personal items, such as letters and documents from his business, has the name Finnegan ever come up?" Murphy said.

"That's the first place I looked when I remembered this a few days ago," Mrs. Miles said. "I could find nothing."

"May we borrow the documents?" Murphy said.

"Certainly."

Mrs. Miles stood up from the table and looked at Knoop. "Would you like some of those cookies to take with you?" she said.

"Finnegan is downtown, but I'd like to go there next," Murphy said.

Matsell leaned in close to the carriage driver. "West 10th Street," he said.

"In the UK, every other family is named Finnegan," Knoop said. "It's quite possible Mr. Miles came across a Finnegan in New York, given the city's large Irish population."

"New York is a big city, but Manhattan is a small island," Murphy said. "It's quite possible, Melvin."

"I wish I could say I knew the man, but the name escapes me," Mrs. Finnegan said. "If my husband knew him, he never mentioned him."

"Are you absolutely sure?" Murphy said.

"I'm sure my husband never mentioned the name Dennis Miles," Mrs. Finnegan said. "If he knew him, he isn't around to say."

"The police reports state he was returning home from work

when he was attacked," Murphy said. "Was that his usual time to get home?"

"Unless the paper ran late," Mrs. Finnegan said. "He was a printer, and the paper usually wrapped around eight in the evening."

"Thank you for your time, Mrs. Finnegan," Murphy said.

"Melvin and I are spending the evening reading the documents we took from Mrs. Miles," Murphy said. "You are welcome to join us, Commissioner."

"I have a department to see to, and this isn't the only matter at hand," Matsell said.

"Have your driver drop us off then," Murphy said.

Knoop munched on almond cookies with a tall glass of milk as he read through the stacks of documents Mrs. Miles gave them to read.

Murphy sat in a leather chair, read, smoked his pipe, and sipped from a glass of whiskey.

"Miles was a meticulous man," Murphy said.

Knoop set a document on the table in the study and reached for the last almond cookie. "I haven't come across even a whisper of the name Finnegan," he said.

Murphy set the document in his hand on the table.

"Miles was definitely a meticulous man," he said.

"According to his financial records, he left his wife thirty thousand dollars in cash, another ten in stock holdings, and an insurance police worth five thousand," Knoop said. "Enough to last her the rest of her life."

"None of which is why he or the others were killed," Murphy said.

Knoop reached into the box of documents. "Do you want a stack of letters or a book marked 'Daily Journal'?"

"Journal."

Knoop handed the journal to Murphy.

"I wish I had more of these cookies," Knoop said.

"If it will tide you over until later, there is still half the apple pie in the icebox," Murphy said.

While Knoop went to the kitchen, Murphy started to read the journal. Miles wrote in the journal daily, most of the posts highlighting his day.

Rose at 4:45. Daily walk from 5:30 to 6:10. Breakfast at 7. Office at 8:15. Lunch at noon. Home at 5:45.

Miles wrote about his day, every day, and most entries in the journal were routine and mundane.

Murphy read each entry, searching for something useful to focus on.

It came the day after Finnegan was shot.

Miles wrote, *Very strange today. At the office I ready the story of a 6th shooting of a man names Francis Finnegan. I had the odd feeling I knew this man from somewhere in the past.*

Murphy looked up at Knoop, who was eating a large slice of apple pie, then continued to read.

Asked my wife at dinner if she knew the name Francis Finnegan. She did not. The eerie feeling that I know this man continues to plague me.

The next ten days in the journal were mostly about his daily routine.

Four days before he was killed, Miles wrote: *As I walked along the river this morning it was still too dark to see clearly at a distance, but I had the feeling a man was following me. He wasn't, of course, but I still had the feeling he was.*

The next two entries were the normal daily routine.

The day before he was shot, Miles wrote: *I believe I saw the same man following me as several days ago. Too dark to see his features. At 69th Street, I turned back and walked toward him. As a precaution I had my .32 revolver at the ready. Before I reached 68th Street, he had turned the corner and disappeared. Very perplexing.*

That was the last entry in the journal.

Miles didn't make another note in his journal after his walk in the park. Obviously, Miles had been shaken up by the episode in the park with the stranger and failed to write any more the day before he died.

"Melvin, read this," Murphy said. "From the day after Finnegan was shot."

Murphy handed Knoop the journal.

While Knoop read, Murphy refilled his shot glass with whiskey and stuffed his pipe with fresh tobacco. He sipped whiskey, struck a match, and lit the pipe.

Suddenly, Knoop looked up at Murphy.

"They missed this," he said. "The city police detectives missed this."

"They spoke with Mrs. Miles before she remembered about Finnegan," Murphy said. "They didn't have a reason to go through all this stuff prior to that."

"He knew he was being followed?" Knoop said. "It proves your theory that it's the work of one man acting alone and with a purpose."

There was a knock on the front door. Murphy stood and walked to the door in time to see a telegram fall through the mail slot. He picked up the telegram and opened it.

Arrived safely at Grant's. Love you, Kai.

Murphy returned to the study where Knoop was reading the journal again.

"Kai arrived safely at the Grants," he said.

"How long will she stay?" Knoop asked.

"Until I send for her."

"Who will do the cooking?" Knoop asked. "I'm terrible in the kitchen."

"We'll figure something out," Murphy said.

"Miles felt strongly about Finnegan," Knoop said. "I wonder if he ever remembered where he remembered him from?"

"He would have written it down and told his wife," Murphy said.

"We need to go back and check Miles and Finnegan's history," Knoop said. "They may have crossed paths, if even briefly. Maybe in business or at an important event or something along those lines."

"If Miles kept one journal a year and Mrs. Miles still has them, we can start with them," Murphy said.

"Agreed," Knoop said.

"Let's go for a walk," Murphy said. "I need some air to clear my head."

"Where are we?" Knoop asked.

"This area is known as Gramercy Park," Murphy said. "We're lucky the gate is unlocked. It usually isn't."

They found a vacant bench and sat. Two women with babies sat on a bench on the other side of the two-acre park.

"We'll need to talk to Commissioner Matsell in the morning and tell him what we've found," Knoop said.

"We'll tell him later, after we visit Mrs. Miles again," Murphy said.

"He won't like that," Knoop said.

Murphy looked at Knoop.

"Right," Knoop said.

A man wearing a suit and accompanied by a boy of about ten entered the park. They walked past Murphy and Knoop, and the man paused, turned around, and walked to Murphy.

"Are you residents?" the man said.

"Of what?" Murphy asked.

"The neighborhood surrounding the park you are sitting in,"

the man said. "This park is for residents only. I'm afraid I'm going to have to ask you to leave."

Murphy stood up and towered over the man. The man's eyes immediately registered that he had made a very big mistake. The boy looked up at Murphy with wide-eyed wonder.

"Are you asking us to leave the park?" Murphy said calmly.

The man's lips quivered a bit. "This park is for private use of residents of the neighborhood. We pay dues to support the upkeep of the park, and it is private property."

Murphy looked at the man, then at the man's son.

"You are correct, sir," Murphy said. "My friend and I didn't realize the park was private property. Come on, Melvin."

Knoop stood and nodded to the man.

On the street, Knoop said, "I've watched you take on five hardened criminals at once and not give it a second thought."

"Melvin, never embarrass a man in front of his young son," Murphy said. "The one you hurt most is the boy."

"Where shall we eat dinner?" Knoop asked.

CHAPTER SEVEN

"Wonderful supper as usual, Julia," Grant said.

"I'll bring your coffee to the study," Julia said.

While Grant went to his study, Julia and Kai washed and put away the crockery.

"It's a lovely evening. Why don't we take coffee on the porch," Julia suggested.

They took cups and a fresh pot to the porch and watched the setting sun.

"What is troubling you, Kai?" Julia said.

"Does it show?" Kai asked.

Julia grinned. "Honey, you wear your heart on your sleeve."

Kai sighed and sipped some coffee. "I'm worried Murphy will get the idea to run for Congress again," she said.

"Is that such a terrible thing?" Julia asked.

"We have the farm in Tennessee, the new home in Fort Smith, and an application to adopt a child," Kai said. "A run for Congress . . . well, it could ruin all of our plans. When an idea takes root in Murphy's mind, the devil himself can't shake it loose."

"I see," Julia said. "Maybe you should talk to Hiram."

Kai looked at Julia. "Mr. Grant?"

"He didn't get to be a general and the president without knowing how to listen," Julia said.

Julia served coffee to Grant and Kai and then said, "I have a few things to do, dear."

After Julia left the study, Grant opened a desk drawer and removed a bottle of bourbon. He added a splash to his cup and then looked at Kai. "Sweetener?" he said.

"Is that Murphy's whiskey?"

"It is," Grant said as he added some to Kai's cup.

Kai lifted her cup. "What shall we drink to, General?"

"Loved ones."

"Loved ones," Kai repeated.

"To loved ones," Grant said and sipped from his cup. He reached for a cigar in the box on his desk and lit it with a wood match. "What Julia told me is that you're upset with the idea Murphy might get it in his head to run for Congress again."

"We're adopting a child. We're building a second home in Fort Smith where I'm supposed to teach school in the Indian Nation," Kai said.

Grant took another sip from his cup. "I've known Murphy since the first year of the war," he said. "No finer friend or more loyal man than Murphy. Now let's just say down the road a ways, Burke comes calling again with the next big crisis. Murphy goes riding off again to who knows where and leaves you behind with a house, a farm, and a child. Murphy is the best lawman I have ever seen, but even Murphy isn't immune to old age. He'll ride off one day and not come back. Will you be able to stop him?"

"No," Kai admitted. "When he believes it's the right thing to do, nothing and nobody can stop him."

"But if he was serving in Congress again, he wouldn't be asked, and Congress is in session only half the year," Grant said. "They may raise their feathers and wave their fists in the air, but nobody is going to shoot at him."

Grant emptied his cup.

"Would you like more coffee, General?" Kai said.

"Why not," Grant said.

Kai lifted the bottle of bourbon and filled Grant's cup.

"I believe I'll go help Julia with her chores," Kai said.

In the study, Murphy poured a small drink of bourbon, lit his pipe, and read Miles's journal again, hoping to see something he'd missed earlier.

I believe I saw the same man following me as several days ago. Too dark to see his features. At 69th Street, I turned back and walked toward him. As a precaution I had my .32 revolver at the ready. Before I reached 68th Street, he had turned the corner and disappeared. Very perplexing.

Miles had believed he saw the same man following him, but he wasn't sure. It was dark, a half hour before dawn, and the man he saw could have been someone else.

That's what a lawyer would claim in court.

Miles never made another entry in his journal. Was he so shaken by seeing the man following him twice that he neglected to make another entry?

Or was there some other reason?

Murphy flipped pages backward.

Asked my wife at dinner if she knew the name Francis Finnegan. She did not. The eerie feeling that I know this man continues to plague me.

Murphy closed the journal and sipped his bourbon.

Something struck him, and he reached for the stack of police reports on Miles. He read each report twice.

Personal belongings found on Miles's body included his wallet and cash, pocket watch, pen knife, wedding band, and snuff case.

The day before he was killed, Miles wrote he was glad he carried his .32 revolver.

The police had made no mention of the revolver in their reports.

What happened to it?

Murphy grabbed the medical examiner's report. Miles was one of two victims who were shot more than once. Shot in the back, the .36 caliber ball lodged in his right lung. The second shot was a direct hit and nicked the heart.

It was the second shot that killed him.

How much time elapsed between shots?

Enough time for Miles to draw and fire his .32 caliber revolver?

Murphy jotted a note to himself.

Recheck clothing worn by Miles.

Ask Mrs. Miles about the .32 when requesting the remaining journals.

Murphy sighed and tossed back the remaining whiskey in his glass,

"Melvin, read the Miles reports one more time," Murphy said.

They were having breakfast at the table in the kitchen. Murphy did the cooking, scrambled eggs, bacon, toast, juice, and coffee.

Knoop flipped pages as he ate.

"What am I looking for?" Knoop asked.

"Read the evidence reports again and tell me what you don't see," Murphy said.

Knoop flipped pages, read, and then looked at Murphy. "The .32 revolver. Where is it?"

"Maybe Mrs. Miles can tell us," Murphy said.

"Are there any more eggs?" Knoop said.

"Driver, let us off here," Murphy said.

Murphy paid the driver, then he and Knoop stepped down

from the carriage on 70th Street one block from the East River.

"Miles was found here on the corner," Murphy said. "But that doesn't mean he was first shot here."

Knoop looked left and then right. "He took the first bullet and could have walked or run an entire block before he was shot the second time."

"More than enough time for Miles to draw his .32 and return fire," Murphy said. "He's hit with the second shot, drops the .32, stumbles to the corner, and falls over dead."

"So what happened to his .32?" Knoop said.

"He could have dropped it in the park by the river, the killer picked it up, a stranger picked it up, the couple out for an early walk that discovered the body picked it up, a bum found it—any or all," Murphy said.

"Let's go see Mrs. Miles," Knoop said.

At the kitchen table, Mrs. Miles poured tea.

"I can make you a pot of coffee if you prefer, but I always drink tea in the morning," she said.

"Tea is fine," Murphy said.

Knoop sipped his tea. "Earl Grey," he said.

"You know your tea, Mr. Knoop," Mrs. Miles said.

"I'm from Scotland," Knoop said.

"Mrs. Miles, we have two important questions," Murphy said. "Do you have your husband's journals from previous years?"

"Oh, dear. Thirty at least," Mrs. Miles said.

"May we borrow them?" Murphy asked.

"Yes, but why? His journals are as dull as week-old soup."

"There might be a reference to Francis Finnegan somewhere in previous years," Murphy said.

Mrs. Miles nodded. "They're in the attic. You'll have to get them. What is the other question?"

"It's about the .32 caliber revolver your husband mentioned in his journal," Murphy said.

"What about it?"

"Do you have it?" Murphy said.

Mrs. Miles seemed taken aback by the question. "Why . . . why no, I don't. I assumed it was recovered with his other possessions the police are holding with the other evidence."

"It's not," Murphy said. "Do you know where he kept it in the house?"

"In his closet on the top shelf, but it isn't there," Mrs. Miles said. "I know. because I selected a burial suit and . . ."

"May we have a look?" Murphy said.

"Yes."

Murphy, Knoop, and Mrs. Miles searched the closets, dressers, and writing desk without results.

"Is it possible the police overlooked it?" Mrs. Miles said.

"We'll ask them," Murphy said. "About the journals."

"The attic."

In the hallway between the bedrooms, Murphy pulled down the section in the ceiling that was actually a staircase to the attic. Mrs. Miles lit a lantern and led Murphy and Knoop up the stairs.

"There. That box in the corner," Mrs. Miles said.

Murphy carried the box down the stairs and closed the attic staircase.

"Would you boys like another cup of tea?" Mrs. Miles asked.

"Where the hell have you boys been?" Matsell said when Murphy and Knoop were ushered into Matsell's office.

"We'll fill you in on the way," Murphy said.

"To where?" Matsell said.

"Evidence warehouse," Murphy said.

★ ★ ★ ★ ★

Murphy took the right sleeve of the suit jacket Miles wore the day he was shot and held it to his nose. He sniffed and then gave it to Knoop.

"Smell," Murphy said.

Knoop took a sniff. "Gunpowder residue," he said.

"Let me see that," Matsell said. He took the jacket from Knoop and sniffed the sleeve.

"After he was shot in the lung, Miles had time to draw and fire his .32 revolver before taking the second, fatal bullet to the heart," Murphy said.

"What happened to the .32?" Matsell said.

"We visited the scene where Miles was killed this morning," Murphy said.

"If the killer is as good a shot as Murphy, he could have shot Miles from seventy-five or even a hundred feet," Knoop said. "Miles still had the capacity to run and even return fire before he was shot the second time. Miles could have fled several hundred feet from where he was initially attacked. He could have dropped the .32 after he fired it or while he was running away.

"I advise that you send a team of men to cover the walking path at the river, the sidewalk, and park within a four-block area," Murphy said.

"I shall, but if we recover the gun, what does it prove?" Matsell asked.

"The killer may have picked up the .32 and tossed it away in the heat of the moment," Murphy said.

"And if he did, we will have his fingerprints," Knoop said.

"His fingerprints?" Matsell said.

"Let us know if they find it," Murphy said.

In the study, Murphy divided the journals into two piles and hunkered down to read them.

After reading five journals from thirty years ago, Murphy closed the fifth one and stood up to stretch his back.

"We've been reading for hours," he said. "Let's take a walk, clear our heads, and get some dinner."

After a brisk walk, Murphy suggested Pete's Tavern, an establishment that opened its doors during the Civil War.

At a table by the front window, Murphy and Knoop ordered steaks.

"Let me toss this out there," Knoop said. "If we do find a connection to Miles and Finnegan from the past, do you think it has anything to do with the other five murders?"

"I've thought that since the beginning," Murphy said. "There is too much planning for these to be random acts, Melvin."

"I agree that they aren't random, but it could be just coincidence that Miles and Finnegan crossed paths in the past," Knoop said.

"I don't believe in coincidence," Murphy said. "I've seen what men can do to each other in war, for money, for hatred, for love and for politics, and it never comes down to coincidence."

"I used to think only evil people committed evil acts," Knoop said. "Since I've worked for Mr. Pinkerton, I've come to realize that good people can do evil when pushed to it, out of desperation."

Murphy nodded as he sliced off a forkful of his steak. "That assignment you're working on for Pinkerton, cataloging photographs. What does he plan to do with it?"

"Take it to Washington before Congress," Knoop said. "He believes such a book of known criminal faces organized for every US marshal and county sheriff to have at their fingertips will help reduce crime across the country."

"If every time a criminal was arrested, they could be

fingerprinted and those fingerprints added to the photographs, a lot of guilty men wouldn't go free," Murphy said.

Knoop stared at Murphy for a moment.

"I'll mention that to Mr. Pinkerton when I get back to Chicago," Knoop said.

"Good," Murphy said. "Now, are you in the mood for dessert?"

When Murphy and Knoop returned to the townhouse, Commissioner Matsell was waiting for them in his carriage.

"I have news," Matsell said.

"Come in for a drink," Murphy said.

In the study, Murphy filled three shot glasses with bourbon and gave one to Knoop and Matsell.

Matsell sipped. "We found the .32 about one block from where Miles was shot, in a clump of bushes on the walking path," he said. "Miles fired two shots."

"Where is the gun now?" Murphy said.

"With my detectives."

Murphy looked at Knoop.

"How many people handled it?" Murphy asked.

"I don't know," Matsell admitted.

"It's probably useless for fingerprints at this point," Murphy said. "Did they find blood anywhere that might indicate if Miles hit the man with one of his two shots?"

"We had several days of hard rain before you arrived, so it's impossible to tell," Matsell said.

"We'll give you our finding as soon as we're through reading these journals," Murphy said.

After Matsell left, Murphy and Knoop spent several more hours reading.

By midnight, Knoop was asleep with his head on the table.

Murphy poured another drink, lit his pipe, sat in a leather

chair, and opened a journal from thirteen years ago.

January, February, and March were much the same mundane writing as in previous journals, but when Murphy got to April he sat up and took notice.

Jury duty begins April 9th.

The next entry was dated the 17th.

Jury duty ends. Back home.

"Melvin, wake up," Murphy said.

When Knoop didn't stir, Murphy stood and shook him awake.

"What time is it?" Knoop asked.

"Twelve-thirty."

"Morning or afternoon?"

"Morning."

"I'm going to bed then."

"Read this first," Murphy said and set the journal in front of Knoop.

Knoop scanned the page.

"Jury duty?" Knoop said as he looked up.

"Tomorrow we revisit Mrs. Finnegan to find out if her husband ever served on a jury," Murphy said. "It might turn out to be your coincidence."

CHAPTER EIGHT

Mrs. Finnegan poured tea in the kitchen for Murphy and Knoop.

"Mrs. Finnegan, did your husband ever serve on a jury?" Murphy asked.

"A jury? Why, yes, about twelve or thirteen years ago, I believe."

"Was he sequestered?" Murphy said.

"Was he what?"

"Not allowed to come home during the trial," Murphy said.

"Yes. For about a week, I believe. He stayed at a hotel somewhere downtown."

"Do you remember the month?"

"March or April," Mrs. Finnegan said. "Why? Is that important?"

After leaving Mrs. Finnegan, Murphy and Knoop met with Commissioner Matsell in Edson's office at City Hall.

Edson and Matsell looked at the journal where Murphy highlighted the entry with a red pencil.

"Jury duty?" Matsell said.

"Both Finnegan and Miles sat on a jury around the same time," Murphy said. "If it was the same jury, it links them together. We'd like to get a warrant to search court records."

"Court records are public knowledge," Edson said.

"Not the names of the jury members," Murphy said.

Edson nodded. "Commissioner, get a judge to issue a warrant to check the court records for jury members."

Matsell, Murphy, and Knoop stood before a superior court judge in his chambers and waited for the judge to sign the warrant.

"I must caution you," the judge said. "If I see any leak to the media, you will stand before me in court. Is that clear to you gentlemen?"

"Judge, we want to stop a killer before he kills again," Matsell said. "We're not interested in publicity."

"Then go do your job," the judge said.

A court clerk in the records office led them to the basement room where transcripts of trials were stored.

"Thirteen years ago. Do you have a month?" the clerk said.

"April," Murphy said.

"Manhattan and southern Westchester County are lumped together," the clerk said. "I'll get the boxes from the catacombs."

The clerk was gone for ten minutes before he returned with three wood boxes full of documents.

"This is half of them," he said.

Murphy carried the last of the six boxes into the study of the townhouse and set them beside the table.

Matsell and Knoop looked at the six boxes.

"This might take a while," Murphy said.

"Two boxes each," Matsell said.

"So you're staying?" Murphy said.

"This is the closest we've come to a genuine lead," Matsell said.

Murphy looked at his pocket watch. "Is your driver still outside?"

"He'll wait until I tell him to go," Matsell said.

"Do you know of a restaurant that can bring our dinner so we don't have to stop working?" Murphy said.

"Delmonico's," Matsell said.

"Have your driver go to Delmonico's in two hours and pick up four steak dinners," Murphy said.

"And pie," Knoop said.

"And pie," Murphy said. "Now, grab a crate."

As Knoop munched on a large slice of apple pie, he read a court document listing the twelve members of a jury.

"Murphy," he said.

Murphy and Matsell stood from their leather chairs and leaned over Knoop's shoulders.

"My God," Matsell said as he read the list of names.

"The seven murdered men sat on this jury," Knoop said.

"That means, if the remaining five members are still alive, they are on the murderer's kill list," Knoop said.

"Did you smudge the list there in the corner?" Murphy asked.

"No, that smudge was already there," Knoop said.

"We need the trial transcript, the judge who presided, and the prosecutor," Murphy said. "And we need to know who was on trial."

"It's in the box," Knoop said. "I separated the jury lists from the transcripts so I could read faster."

Murphy dug through the stack of folders and found the transcript that matched the list of jury names.

He took his leather chair and read aloud.

"John Stuyvesant was arrested in 1869 for the murder of his wife, Abigail. He shot her once in the head with a Colt .36 caliber revolver, the revolver he carried in the Civil War from 1862 until it ended," Murphy said. "While Stuyvesant was away from home, his wife began an affair with an older man, a banker named Gruber. Upon his return, Abigail continued the secret affair with Gruber and, in 1868, she gave birth to a son. Gruber's son."

"How did she know it wasn't Stuyvesant's?" Matsell said.

"According to his statement to the police, Stuyvesant, who has blond hair and blue eyes, as does his wife, first became suspicious when the child was born with dark hair and eyes. After one year, the child's hair was even darker, as were the eyes. Stuyvesant took to spying on his wife and following her. He eventually found them together in Gruber's townhouse on 21st Street and First Avenue. He broke in, shot his wife once in the head, Gruber once in the chest, and then left. He walked to the nearest police station and turned himself in."

"I remember that case," Matsell said. "I was a captain in Harlem at the time."

"Although Stuyvesant's defense attorney painted Stuyvesant as a victim of circumstances and played on the all-male jury's sympathies, Stuyvesant was found guilty of murder. He received twelve to twenty-five years in prison."

"Who were the judge and prosecutor?" Matsell asked.

"Judge was W. Carey, and the prosecutor was Thomas Griffin," Murphy said.

"I need to find out where the remaining five members of the jury are, along with the judge and the prosecutor," Matsell said.

"First find out if Stuyvesant was paroled," Murphy said.

"Of course," Matsell said. "I'll have my driver take me to my office and send telegrams at once."

"If this information is accurate, and I believe that it is, seven more men are on Stuyvesant's list," Murphy said.

"After I send the telegrams, I shall meet with the mayor at his residence," Matsell said. "Do you wish to accompany me?"

"Pick us up on the way back," Murphy said. "We still have some notes to make."

After Matsell left, Murphy said, "Melvin, pour us a drink of my father's whiskey and then take some notes."

Knoop filled two shot glasses with whiskey, sat at the table, and waited with pencil in hand.

"The remaining five members of the jury are David Clinton, Donald Craig, Robert E. Wood, John James Olson, and J. Douglas Turner," Murphy said. "The prosecutor was Thomas Griffin, and the judge was W. Carey."

Knoop scribbled nearly as quickly as Murphy dictated.

"Add this," Murphy said. "Defense attorney was Michael Laugher. Stuyvesant could also be holding a grudge against his own attorney."

Knoop added Laugher's name to the list.

Murphy lit his pipe. "Our assignment is close to being concluded," he said.

"Stuyvesant is still at large," Knoop said.

"I was asked to help the police identify a sequential killer and I've done so," Murphy said. "The rest is up to the police."

Knoop sipped his drink. "After I send a report to Mr. Pinkerton, he'll probably send for me," he said.

"But you'd like to stay?"

"I would like to see Stuyvesant caught, yes," Knoop said.

"Maybe Pinkerton will let you," Murphy said.

"But not you?"

"Kai would not like that, Melvin," Murphy said.

"No, I suppose not," Knoop said.

"Well, I'm going to clean up a bit and change my shirt before we see the mayor," Murphy said.

Edson received Matsell, Murphy, and Knoop in the study of his residence on the East Side. He wore a red robe over his pajamas as he took the chair behind his desk.

"Pour us all a drink, would you?" he said to Matsell.

Matsell went to the bar, poured four drinks, and carried them on a tray to the desk.

"Now what's this all about?" Edson said.

Matsell looked at Murphy. "It's only fitting you make the initial report," he said.

Murphy spoke for about ten minutes and then showed Edson the court documents.

"We don't know about Judge Carey or the two lawyers involved in the trial at this point," Murphy said after he concluded his report. "The commissioner is handling that part."

Edson downed his shot of whiskey and looked at Matsell.

"Judge Carey retired from the bench five years ago," Matsell said. "I don't know where he resides at the moment, but we will track him down in the morning. Defense attorney Laugher passed away four years ago, and Prosecutor Thomas Griffin has left the city. We don't know where he is at the moment or if he is even still practicing law."

"Find out," Edson said. "First thing in the morning."

"Yes, sir," Matsell said.

"Mr. Murphy, Mr. Knoop, will you be staying on as advisors?" Edson said.

"I won't be," Murphy said. "I have other matters to attend to."

"If Mr. Pinkerton will allow it, I would like to stay on as an advisor," Knoop said.

"Very well then," Edson said. "Commissioner, in my office first thing in the morning."

"Melvin, in the morning, how would you like to take a carriage ride?" Murphy asked when he and Knoop returned to the townhouse.

"To where?" Knoop said.

"It's time you met General Grant," Murphy said.

CHAPTER NINE

Matsell arrived at the townhouse while Murphy and Knoop were having breakfast.

He took coffee with them in the kitchen.

"Stuyvesant was paroled thirteen months ago and returned to Manhattan to live with his sister," Matsell said. "Her married name is Finch. She lives in a building on 155th Street and Eighth Avenue. We're on our way there now, if you'd like to accompany us."

Knoop looked at Murphy. "I'd like to," he said.

"Have you located Judge Carey and Prosecutor Griffin?" Murphy said.

"I have a team of detectives working on that right now," Matsell said.

"We'll take a ride with you," Murphy said.

"My husband is at work," Katherine Finch said as she poured coffee in the kitchen. "My son Adam often goes to work with his father when school is not in session."

"Adam is your brother's son, isn't that so?" Murphy said.

Katherine hung her head for a moment and then looked up. "Adam doesn't know that," she said.

"And he won't," Murphy said. "That's not why we're here."

Katherine nodded.

"What does your husband do?" Matsell said.

"He works for the dairy on 170th Street," Katherine said.

"Deliveries five days a week. But you said you're here about my brother."

"We'd like to talk to him," Murphy said. "Do you know where he is right now?"

"I saw my brother for two days after he was paroled," Katherine said. "I warned him not to marry a woman who wasn't a virgin, but he wouldn't listen. He was in love. Why, the woman flirted with my own husband at Thanksgiving supper. I spoke with her in private, and she told me she had an itch below the waist that needed constant scratching. She was nothing but a common whore, that one."

"After your brother came to see you, what happened?" Murphy said.

"He was here for two days," Katherine said. "He said he came to collect what was his. We kept a trunk with his personal possessions for him. He picked up what he wanted and said he was leaving this city for good."

"What did he take, do you remember?" Murphy asked.

"Clothes. Three thousand dollars in gold coin. He left me one thousand dollars in paper money. He hated paper money."

"Did he have a weapon in the trunk?" Murphy said.

"He returned home from the war with two Navy Colts," Katherine said. "They were his prized possessions. The police took one when he surrendered to them. The other was in the trunk. He took that when he left."

Murphy looked at Knoop and Matsell.

"Why? What is it you think my brother has done?" Katherine said.

"Have you read about the recent killings in the streets?" Murphy said. "Each man was killed with a .36 caliber Navy Colt, exactly like the one your brother took from the trunk."

Katherine stared at Murphy.

"That can't be," she said. "Why would my brother kill innocent strangers on the street for no reason?"

"He had a reason," Murphy said. "Those men were members of the jury that sent him to prison."

Katherine gasped.

"Do you have any idea where he might be?" Murphy asked.

"He said . . . he said he was leaving the city," Katherine said.

"Have you heard from him since?" Murphy said.

"No, not a word," Katherine said. "They stuck him in a prison in Ohio. I couldn't even visit him, but I wrote twice a month. Sometimes he wrote back."

"Mrs. Finch, what we just discussed is a highly classified police matter," Matsell said. "I must insist that you not discuss this with anyone, not even your husband."

Katherine nodded. "I feel suddenly quite ill," she said.

"Understandable," Matsell said. "We shall leave you now."

Riding back in Matsell's carriage, Murphy said, "Contact the prison where Stuyvesant was incarcerated and find out what kind of prisoner he was. Also, ask the army for his military records."

"That will take the rest of the day into tonight," Matsell said. "What with all the other things we need to do."

"No problem," Murphy said. "Knoop and I are going for a ride to the country."

When Murphy stopped the buggy in front of Grant's home in Point Pleasant, Kai and Julia were having tea on the porch.

Before Murphy and Knoop exited the buggy, Kai was off the porch and by Murphy's side.

She hugged him tightly, and then broke free and hugged Knoop.

"Why didn't you wire?" she said.

"I wanted to surprise you," Murphy said. "Melvin, may I

present Julia Grant, former First Lady of the United States."

Knoop stared at Julia Grant, who smiled at him from the porch.

"Have you had lunch?" Julia said.

"So, Marvin, you're an agent for Pinkerton's?" Grant said.

"Yes, sir, and it's Melvin, sir. Melvin Knoop," Knoop said.

"Of course it is," Grant said.

Murphy grinned as he cut into a thick slice of roast beef.

"What do you do for Pinkerton's?" Grant asked.

"Forensic science and investigations, Mr. President," Knoop said.

"Sounds fascinating," Grant said.

"It is, sir," Knoop said. "Murphy and I just discovered the man committing those murders in New York City."

Kai glanced at Murphy.

"The one using an old Navy Colt?" Grant said.

"Yes, sir. It turns out the man was sentenced to prison for killing his wife and her lover with an old Navy Colt," Knoop said. "He was paroled and is now murdering the members of the jury that convicted him."

"But the man is still at large?" Grant said.

"For the moment," Knoop said.

Kai looked at Murphy again.

"Will you be assisting the police in his capture?" Grant said.

"I hope to, sir," Knoop said. "Murphy plans to return home, but I would like to stay and assist the police as an advisor."

Kai looked at Murphy one more time. "Good choice," she whispered.

After lunch, Kai and Murphy took a walk along the tree-lined street.

Knoop stayed behind to talk with Grant.

Knoop had a hundred questions about the war and Grant's

time in the White House.

"Mr. President, may I ask you a personal question about Murphy?" Knoop asked.

"Murphy is the one you should direct personal questions to if they concern him," Grant said.

"He won't tell me, sir," Knoop said. "What his first name is."

"I see," Grant said. "Now, Marvin, have—"

"It's Melvin, sir," Knoop said.

"Of course it is," Grant said. "Now, Melvin, have you ever seen what Murphy can do to a man when he has a mind to?"

"Some, sir," Knoop said. "He's quite formidable when provoked."

"I wouldn't pester him about his name if I were you," Grant said. "Just a word of caution."

"So you've decided to come home with me then?" Kai said.

"I did what was asked of me," Murphy said. "We need to return to Fort Smith and see to our house and then get in touch with the adoption agency."

"So are you asking me to pack?" Kai said.

"I guess I am," Murphy said.

Kai paused and looked up at Murphy.

"Burke will return when things don't go well," she said. "We both know that."

Murphy and Grant shook hands on the porch. Julia hugged Kai and then kissed Murphy on the cheek.

Grant shook hands with Knoop.

"Remember what I told you, Marvin," Grant said.

"It's . . . never mind. I will remember, Mr. President," Knoop said.

Murphy drove the buggy. Knoop sat to Kai's right and she linked arms with him.

"What did Grant tell you?" Kai asked Knoop.

Knoop leaned in close to Kai's ear and whispered.

Kai looked at Knoop.

"He gave you good advice," she said. "I'd follow it."

In the living room of the townhouse, Murphy studied the railroad schedule.

He stood and went to the bedroom on the second floor.

"There is a train to Fort Smith tomorrow at noon," he said.

Kai was packing her luggage on the bed.

"I need a bath," she said. "In fact, we both do."

Kai removed her skirt and blouse and walked to the private room where the tub was located. She paused and looked back at Murphy.

"Are you coming?" she said.

"Hell, yes," Murphy said.

"Commissioner," Knoop said when he answered the door.

"I have some new information," Matsell said.

"Come in," Knoop said.

"Where is Murphy?"

"I think he's taking a bath."

When her breathing returned to normal, Kai said, "I take it you missed me."

Murphy looked at Kai.

"It's okay. The big, tough man can say it," Kai said.

"Hell, Kai," Murphy said.

Kai grinned. "You can do it. It will only hurt for a moment. Honest."

"All right, I missed you," Murphy said.

"Good. Now get off me before you bust my ribs," Kai said.

Murphy rolled over and sat up on the bed just as there was a knock on the door.

"Murphy, it's Melvin. Commissioner Matsell is here with some news," Knoop said from the hallway.

Murphy sighed. "Be right there, Melvin," he said.

"What did you find out?" Murphy asked Matsell when he entered the living room.

"Which do you want to see first, his prison record or his military record?" Matsell said.

"Prison."

Murphy took the file, sat on the sofa and began to read.

After his conviction, Stuyvesant was sent to a federal prison in Ohio to serve his time. He kept to himself and was, by all accounts, a model prisoner. During the first two years of his stay, he worked in the cobbler shop, making shoes and boots. In his fourth year, he worked as a blacksmith, making shoes for the army. In his fifth year, Stuyvesant became a trustee and remained so until his parole during his twelfth year of incarceration. Upon his parole, Stuyvesant was sent home with a new suit of clothes, two hundred dollars, and a railroad ticket to Manhattan.

Murphy closed the file.

"Let's have us a drink, Melvin," he said.

Knoop filled three shot glasses and gave one to Murphy and Matsell.

Murphy opened the second folder.

Stuyvesant enlisted in the Union Army in the spring of 1862. He fought in several small skirmishes leading up to Gettysburg. During the fighting at Gettysburg, he saved the lives of six soldiers by carrying them on his back from the battlefield to safety, despite being wounded himself. After a brief stay at a hospital, Stuyvesant returned to duty under General "Fighting Joe" Hooker and then General Meade. He rose to the rank of sergeant and stayed an extra six months after the surrender to help with the reconstruction of the South.

He was discharged in early sixty-six and returned home to Manhattan.

Murphy closed the file.

"The man was a decorated soldier," he said.

"Was," Matsell said. "Mr. Knoop, I spoke with the mayor, and he's agreed that you may stay on as an advisor until Stuyvesant is apprehended."

Knoop looked at Murphy.

Murphy shook his head.

"I'll have a carriage pick you up at eight-thirty tomorrow morning," Matsell said.

Matsell extended his right hand to Murphy. Murphy stood, and they shook.

After Matsell left, Murphy said, "I think I'll take Kai to dinner. Feel like accompanying us?"

As Murphy sliced in a dish of baked chicken, he looked across the table at Knoop and said, "Melvin, consider this. The names on the jury list match the first seven victims. That leaves the judge and prosecutor also as potential victims. Consider how Stuyvesant came by the list."

Knoop, about to raise his fork to his mouth, paused. "I hadn't given that much thought," he said.

Kai looked at Murphy. "You have, though," she said.

Knoop looked at Kai. "Is there any way you'd—"

"Kai and I are taking the noon train to Fort Smith in the morning," Murphy said. "But you can ponder with Matsell how Stuyvesant obtained the list."

Knoop nodded.

"Can I come for a visit when this is over?" he asked.

Kai smiled at Knoop. "Of course, Melvin. Any time. So long

as Burke, the president, or Pinkerton's isn't involved."

"Who wants dessert?" Murphy asked.

"Grant seems to think you'll run for Congress again," Kai said as she flipped down the bed covers.

"I'm not going to," Murphy said as he removed his pants.

"But you're thinking about it," Kai said.

"I wasn't," Murphy said as he unbuttoned his shirt.

"You need to tell me these things if we're to make plans," Kai said.

"There is . . . why does Grant think that?" Murphy said.

"He said once the bug bites you it never leaves, or something like that."

"Grant said that?"

"Yes. Is he right?"

Murphy got into bed. "It's something to consider for the future."

Kai got into bed next to Murphy. "You need to tell me these things if we're to make plans," she said.

"I will."

"Good. Be a dear and turn off the lantern."

CHAPTER TEN

After breakfast, Knoop said goodbye to Kai and Murphy and then waited on the sidewalk for Matsell's carriage to arrive.

When the carriage arrived with Matsell as a passenger, Murphy emerged from the townhouse and placed his right hand on Knoop's shoulder.

"Stay with Kai," Murphy said. "If I'm not back by ten-thirty, take Kai to the railroad station and I'll meet you there."

"But . . ."

"Thanks, Melvin," Murphy said.

Murphy went to the carriage, climbed aboard, and sat next to Matsell.

"I don't understand," Matsell said. "I thought you were—"

"I'll explain on the way," Murphy said.

"The way to where?"

"The courthouse, and tell the driver to hurry. I have a train to catch."

"What did you . . . ?" the clerk said.

Murphy entered the office of the records clerk, followed by Matsell.

At his desk, the clerk said, "I remember you from the—"

"Stand up," Murphy said.

"What did you—?" the clerk said.

Murphy grabbed the clerk by the shirt and yanked him to his feet.

"How much?" Murphy said.

"How much what?" the clerk said.

Murphy yanked the clerk across the desk and tossed him to the floor.

"Seven people have been murdered in cold blood, with possibly another six on the way. How much did Stuyvesant pay you for the jury list?" Murphy said.

"I don't know what you're—" the clerk said.

Murphy smacked the clerk across the face, spinning his head.

"I'll ask you again, and then I will beat you to death right here and now if you don't answer," Murphy said.

"Commissioner, are you going to allow him to do this?" the clerk said.

"He's federal. I'm not," Matsell said.

"I'm going to count to three starting with two," Murphy said. "Two."

"Five hundred dollars," the clerk said. "He paid me five hundred dollars for the list."

Murphy released the clerk.

"I didn't know what he was going to use it for, and that's the truth," the clerk said.

"And you didn't stop to think why before you allowed yourself to be bribed?" Murphy said.

"A twelve-year-old jury list? I needed the money. I figured what could it hurt?" the clerk said.

"Now you know what it could hurt," Murphy said. "Commissioner?"

Matsell stepped forward. "You're under arrest for extortion, receiving a bribe, and a few other charges I'll think of later."

The clerk looked at Murphy. "How?"

"Of all the court documents in the six boxes, the jury list was the only one that was smudged," Murphy said. "You're the only one who has access. You must have leaned on it when you copied it for Stuyvesant."

"Damn my bad luck," the clerk said.

"From where I stand, your bad luck is called stupidity," Murphy said.

Murphy arrived at the railroad station a few minutes past eleven. Knoop and Kai were seated on a bench in the waiting room.

"What happened?" Knoop asked.

"Matsell will tell you all about it. He's waiting outside," Murphy said.

Knoop and Kai stood up.

"Goodbye, Melvin," Kai said. "Don't be a stranger. Our door is always open."

Kai hugged Knoop and kissed him on the cheek. When they separated, Knoop had a tear in his eye.

Murphy extended his right hand to Knoop and they shook.

"You might want to check for the court clerk's fingerprints on the jury list," Murphy said. "I didn't have time."

"I will," Knoop said.

Murphy and Kai watched Knoop walk away and out of the waiting room. Kai wiped a small tear from her left eye and then said, "We have a train to catch."

Murphy picked up the luggage and followed Kai to the boarding area.

As the train rolled out of the station, Kai watched from her window seat. Next to her, Murphy read a New York newspaper.

Kai turned and looked at Murphy.

"The schedule says we reach Fort Smith by nine tonight," Kai said. "I reserved a table for dinner at six, but we can get a bite to eat when the car opens for lunch at two."

Murphy lowered the newspaper. "I reserved a sleeping car in

case you want to take a nap."

"A nap?" Kai said. "Oh, a nap. Well, I guess I am a bit sleepy."

Under the covers in the bed in the sleeping car, Kai nestled her face into Murphy's chest.

"I hope Melvin will be all right alone in New York," she said.

"He's not alone," Murphy said. "He's with the entire New York City Police Department."

"But he will be by himself in that townhouse."

"He lives alone in Chicago. Chicago is also a big city. Knoop will be fine."

"I hope so," Kai said. "He is so helpless on his own."

"Knoop is a trained forensics investigator," Murphy said. "An agent of Pinkerton's. He will be fine. Would you rather I stayed with him?"

"No, of course not," Kai said. "That doesn't mean I can't worry about him."

"Worry about him if you must, but he'll be fine," Murphy said. "Since you brought up running for Congress again, I—"

"I didn't bring it up," Kai said.

"The other day," Murphy said.

"Are you considering it?"

"Maybe for Fort Smith," Murphy said. "Since we will be living there while you teach school, it might be something I can pursue. If Judge Parker throws his support behind me, I just might take a run at it."

"If this is something you want to do, just so long as you understand I am not pushing you," Kai said.

"I'll think on it some more," Murphy said.

"Good. Now I'm going to take a real nap," Kai said.

As Murphy carried the luggage from the platform to the dirt streets of Fort Smith, Kai walked by his side and took several deep breaths of the cool, night air.

"I can sleep with the window open tonight," she said.

"Was New York that bad?" Murphy asked.

"That depends on if you enjoy the aroma of wet skunk in your nose twenty-four hours a day," Kai said.

They walked past the courthouse, turned down a side street, and headed to Kai's boarding house. A year ago she hired a woman to run it for her, but Kai kept a room for her and Murphy to stay in when visiting Fort Smith.

"She left a lantern lit on the porch," Kai said.

"And I hope a snack on the table," Murphy said.

Murphy sat on the bed, ate a slice of apple pie, washed it down with a glass of cold milk, and watched Kai brush her hair at the dressing table.

"Mrs. Leary knows how to bake a pie," he said.

"Now that our house is nearly complete, I was thinking I should sell the boarding house to her," Kai said. "What do you think?"

"Can she afford to buy it?" Murphy asked.

"If I sell it cheap enough, the bank will give her a good rate," Kai said.

"Ask her in the morning," Murphy said.

"Can we check with the adoption agency?" Kai said.

"We'll send them a wire before we ride out to see the house," Murphy said.

Kai set the brush aside, stood, and removed her robe. "Would you rather be with Melvin trying to find the killer?" she said.

"I am where I would rather be right now," Murphy said.

"Help me turn down the bed," Kai said.

Wearing a long nightshirt, Knoop sat at the desk in the study and poured over his notes and paperwork.

He drank a glass of milk and nibbled on some cookies as he read and made notes.

The knock on the front door startled him. He stood, left the study, and walked along the hallway to the door.

"Yes, who is there?" Knoop said as he stood behind the heavy, wood door.

"Commissioner Matsell."

Knoop unlocked the door and opened it.

"I know it's late, but I have some news."

"I was up reading," Knoop said. "In the study."

Matsell followed Knoop to the study.

"Would you like a glass of cold milk?" Knoop said.

"I would, actually."

Knoop lifted the steel pitcher on the desk, filled a glass for Matsell, and handed it to him.

"Are those sugar cookies?" Matsell asked.

"Yes, from the bakery on 14th Street," Knoop said. "Help yourself."

Matsell and Knoop sat and each took a cookie.

"Judge Carey retired from the bench five years ago and left New York to live in New Hampshire," Matsell said. "In a town called Laconia. It's a small town not far from the White Mountains. I plan to leave for Laconia tomorrow. Would you like to accompany me and speak to the judge?"

"Of course," Knoop said.

"I'll pick you up at eight," Matsell said. "We'll catch the ten o'clock train for Connecticut and switch to the Merrimack and Connecticut Railroad to Manchester. We'll rent a carriage for the trip to Laconia. Pack for at least overnight or even two days."

"Why this town Laconia?" Knoop asked.

"My research shows that Carey was born there and had family property," Matsell said. "I sent a wire to Western Union to inform him I would be coming to see him. I said his life is in danger and to put a police detail on him for protection. I expect a response by morning."

"What of the remaining jury members?"

"I have a team of men trying to locate them," Matsell said. "We haven't been able to find any of them as yet."

"I better pack and get to bed," Knoop said. "Let's have another cookie first."

After returning from the livery stables with a rented buggy, Murphy entered the boarding house and found Kai waiting for him in the parlor.

Mrs. Leary, the woman entrusted to run the boarding house, and Kai were having tea.

"Mrs. Leary has agreed to buy the boarding house," Kai said. "She and I will go to the bank this afternoon when we return from looking at the house."

"Very good," Murphy said. "Kai, there's a chill this morning. Best grab your wrap."

While Kai went upstairs, Murphy said, "Mrs. Leary, have you the money for a down payment?"

"No, but Kai said she would speak to the loan office on my behalf," Mrs. Leary said.

"I will give you the money for the down payment if you promise to keep it our secret," Murphy said.

"Heavens, why?" Mrs. Leary said.

"So that Kai doesn't," Murphy said. "Tell the loan officer you have the down payment. Agreed?"

"I don't know what to say."

"Nothing. Say nothing. Here comes Kai."

Knoop waited outside the townhouse for Matsell to arrive. He had a packed suitcase by his side. Matsell was twenty minutes late. Just as Knoop was about to hail a passing taxi, Matsell's carriage arrived.

"Sorry I'm late," Matsell said. "I'll explain on the way."

Two carpenters were doing finishing work on the kitchen cabinets and two more were installing floors in the bedrooms.

"It's a beautiful home," Kai said as she stood in the spacious living room. "The kind of home a child could grow up in."

"It should be about another week before you can move in," a carpenter said.

"Do the pumps work?" Murphy asked.

"Give them a try," the carpenter said.

"I want to see everything," Kai said.

"Go ahead," Murphy said. "I'll have a look outside."

Murphy went outside and picked a spot on which to build a corral for his horse, Boyle. To the rear of the house was a nice flat piece of ground where the barn would go. He walked about three hundred feet to the creek running through the property. The water level was high, and he could see trout swimming downstream.

Murphy took out his pipe, stuffed it with fresh tobacco, lit it with a wood match, and sat in the shade of a tree beside the creek.

A fish jumped.

Kai came and sat beside him.

"It's perfect. All we need is a child," she said.

"And furniture," Murphy said.

Kai laughed. "And furniture."

"We can stop by the general store and see what they have in the catalogs," Murphy said. "Since the house isn't ready and it will be weeks before the furniture is delivered, let's head to Tennessee and see my folks."

"See your horse, is what you mean," Kai said.

"And my horse," Murphy admitted.

"Let's head back to town," Kai said. "I need to meet Mrs. Leary at the bank and then wire the adoption agency."

"I thought we might go for a swim," Murphy said. "The creek is high and warm enough."

"There are men in the house," Kai said.

"Don't tell me the Navajo in you is now civilized," Murphy said.

Kai looked at Murphy and then slowly her lips formed a smile.

"Last one in washes the dirty dishes tonight," she said as she unbuttoned her blouse.

Knoop read the lengthy telegram from the sheriff's department of Belknap County where Laconia was located. Judge Carey had been murdered in his home two days ago. Suspect was still at large.

"That's it. That's all the information provided?" Knoop said.

"We'll get the rest in person," Matsell said.

"We're still going to Laconia then?" Knoop said.

"How else are we going to get all the details?" Matsell said.

Murphy escorted Kai and Mrs. Leary to the bank and left them with the loan officer.

From the bank, he walked to the courthouse.

Judge Parker was in his chambers when Murphy was announced by a deputy marshal.

"You're back from New York," Parker said as he stood up from his desk.

"Last night," Murphy said.

"And how did it go?"

"We identified the murderer. That's all I signed up for."

"Grab two glasses from the table. I have a bottle of your

father's whiskey in my desk," Parker said.

Murphy scooped up two shot glasses from the round table beside the window while Parker fished out the bottle of whiskey from his desk.

Parker filled both shot glasses.

Murphy picked up his glass, as did Parker, and both men downed their shots.

"Sit for a minute," Parker said. "Something I'd like to discuss with you."

Murphy took the leather chair facing the desk while Parker took his chair behind it.

"Much of Arkansas is still lawless country," Parker said. "North of the Indian Nation it's still unsettled and wide open. Since you'll be living here most of the year and Kai will start teaching on the reservation soon, I'd like to appoint you a full US marshal. She'd feel better if you didn't have to leave the state and were home most nights."

"I've been thinking on something else, Judge," Murphy said. "I've been thinking of taking a run at Congress again, but out of Arkansas instead of Tennessee. I was hoping to get your endorsement."

"You'll have more than my endorsement," Parker said. "You'll have whatever else I can do before the next election."

"I appreciate it, Judge," Murphy said. "The house should be ready in two weeks or so. How about being our first guest to dinner?"

"That sounds fine," Parker said.

"Well, I left Kai and Mrs. Leary at the bank," Murphy said. "I'd best see to them."

"Did everything turn out all right?" Murphy asked when Kai and Mrs. Leary came out of the bank and met him on the wooden sidewalk.

Mrs. Leary looked at Murphy. "The bank approved the mortgage," she said.

"Excellent," Murphy said.

"I better get back to the house and get started on dinner for the guests," Mrs. Leary said.

"We have some shopping to do," Kai said. "We'll see you back at the house."

As Knoop and Matsell walked along the streets of Manchester, New Hampshire, Matsell said, "I was expecting a small New England town, but Manchester is larger than I thought it would be."

"It must be all these mills," Knoop said.

"We won't make Laconia tonight," Matsell said. "Best find a hotel and livery to rent a carriage for the morning."

As Kai wrote catalog numbers onto the order page, she said, "What do you think of this table and chairs for the kitchen?"

Murphy glanced at the page. "It's fine."

"Better be sure. We're going to have to live with it."

Murphy looked again. "It's fine."

Kai flipped pages in the catalog and, without looking at Murphy, said, "I was surprised at the bank today when Mrs. Leary said she had the down payment on the house."

"She saved her money," Murphy said.

"Or yours," Kai said.

"What do they have in that book for the bedroom?" Murphy said.

CHAPTER ELEVEN

After breakfast and after the guests cleared out, Kai washed and stacked the dirty dishes and then put a kettle on the stove for some tea. When the tea was ready, she carried a tray with pot and cups to the sitting room where Mrs. Leary sat at the window.

From outside, Kai could hear the steady chopping of wood.

"Mrs. Leary, I made some tea," Kai said.

"Does he ever get tired?" Mrs. Leary asked.

Kai set the tray on the table in front of the sofa.

"If he does, it never shows," Kai said.

Kai poured tea, and they sat on the sofa.

"Your husband put up the deposit on the house," Mrs. Leary said. "He would be angry with me if he knew I told you."

"I already figured it out," Kai said.

"He's a good man," Mrs. Leary said.

"Yes, he is," Kai said.

"Don't lose him."

"I'll do my best not to," Kai said.

Shirtless, sweat dripping down his chest and arms, Murphy swung the ax and split a log into two pieces.

Since breakfast, he'd split about a cord.

As he set another log on the block, Judge Parker said, "Hold on a minute, Murphy."

Murphy turned and then set the ax aside.

Parker held a briefcase, opened it, and removed some documents.

"Official documents needed to file to run for Congress," Parker said. "Fill them out when you're ready, and I'll send them off to Washington."

"Thanks, Judge. Why not come in the house for some coffee?"

"I'm due in court, but I'll stop by later and we can talk about filing the papers," Parker said.

The ride to Laconia from Manchester took about five hours by carriage. Matsell and Knoop reached Laconia just after one in the afternoon.

It was a much smaller town than Manchester, with a population of about thirty-five hundred residents.

Matsell located the town sheriff's office on Main Street.

"Judge Carey had a large house on Lake Winnipesaukee," Sheriff Wagner said with a thick, New England twang. "His family goes back five generations or more. It was quite the shock to everyone around here, what happened to him."

"We'd like to check the house for forensics," Knoop said.

"What kind of forensics?" Wagner asked.

"We won't know until we see the house," Knoop said.

"I'll have my driver take us there," Wagner said. "It's about thirty minutes from here."

After lunch, Kai and Murphy sat on the porch with cups of coffee, and together they read the documents needed to file to run for Congress.

"They've made some changes to the filing papers since I last filed," Murphy said.

"Are you sure this is what you want to do?" Kai asked.

"No, I'm not sure," Murphy said. "But I am considering it."

A Western Union courier arrived at the porch. "I'm looking for a Mr. Murphy," he said.

"I'm Murphy," Murphy said.

"Telegram for you, sir," the courier said.

Murphy signed for the telegram and tipped the courier a dollar.

"It's from Burke," he said.

"Damn that man," Kai said.

"Let's see what he wants before you condemn him," Murphy said.

Murphy opened the telegram and read it quickly. "The judge who tried the case involving the man killing the jury members has been killed at his retirement residence in New Hampshire. Knoop and Commissioner Matsell have gone to New Hampshire to investigate," he said.

"And he's asking you to do what?" Kai asked.

"Nothing," Murphy said and handed Kai the telegram. "Not a thing."

As they walked to the front door of Judge Carey's lakeside home, Sheriff Wagner said, "The judge and his family were regular summer fixtures on the lake for thirty years or more. Mrs. Carey and the children would spend the entire summer, and the judge would come up for several weeks between July and August."

They reached the front door and Wagner used a key to unlock it. "After Mrs. Carey died three years ago, the judge retired from the bench and moved here permanently."

Wagner opened the door, and they entered the foyer of the house.

"Wait," Knoop said before Wagner closed the door.

Knoop inspected the lock, the doorframe, and the door itself, and then said, "No sign the door was forced or the lock was picked open."

"How can you tell if a lock was picked?" Wagner asked.

"By the scratch marks," Knoop said. "How many other doors are there?"

"One in the rear and French doors in the master bedroom," Wagner said.

"Show me those first," Knoop said.

Knoop inspected the rear door that went from the kitchen to the backyard and then the French doors that went from the bedroom to the backyard.

"No signs of forced entry or the locks being picked," Knoop said. "Where was the body found, and who found it?"

Wagner took them to Carey's study. It was furnished with a well-stacked bookcase, desk, sofa, table, and bar.

"The judge was writing a letter at the desk when he was shot," Wagner said. "He must have heard the intruder, turned, and was shot once in the chest with a .36 caliber ball."

Knoop inspected the bloodstains on the hardwood floor beside the desk.

"The bullet wound was fatal, but he didn't die instantly," Knoop said. "He fell to the floor and bled for quite a while. Who discovered the body?"

"The housekeeper, at seven the next morning," Wagner said.

"Does the medical examiner know the time of death?" Knoop said.

"Medical examiner?" Wagner said. "We have four doctors in town and every one of them is over sixty and two are drunkards."

"Did they guess as to the time of death?" Knoop said.

"Nine fifty-two in the evening," Wagner said.

"That a pretty precise guess," Knoop said.

"His pocket watch broke when he hit the floor," Wagner said.

"That's when his watch broke," Knoop said. "He could have lingered for quite some time after that."

"That's possible," Wagner said.

"He was alone in the house?" Knoop asked.

"Yes. The housekeeper leaves around four, and the judge always prepared his own supper," Wagner said. "That's what the housekeeper told us."

"Were all doors locked when the housekeeper arrived?" Knoop asked.

"The French doors were unlocked," Wagner said. "The housekeeper has her own key and let herself in," Wagner said. "She said she was in the house about an hour before she discovered the body. She thought the judge was still in bed until she went to clean the study."

"I want to see the grounds," Knoop said.

They returned to the bedroom and entered the garden through the French doors. The backyard took up about a half an acre, protected by a wood fence that stood six feet high. Beyond the fence was the lake.

"The fence has no doors," Knoop said.

"Correct. On the left side of the house is a garden path to the lake," Wagner said.

"Did your men inspect the outside of the fence?" Knoop asked.

"We did, but it rained after midnight that night and continued until morning," Wagner said. "Any footprints were washed away."

"Let's check for evidence," Knoop said.

"Evidence of what?" Wagner said. "The judge was shot with a .36 caliber ball, something I haven't seen in ten years."

"As I said in my telegram, the judge's murder is directly linked to an investigation we are conducting in New York," Matsell said.

"Maybe it's time you explained that," Wagner said.

"I'll be outside," Knoop said.

Knoop left the house, walked around to the rear, and carefully inspected the fence. The ground around the fence was soft dirt and the recent rain had washed away footprints, if there were any.

Knoop was a short man, about five foot, five inches tall and would not be able to scale the fence without assistance. He didn't know how tall Stuyvesant was, but even if he stood six feet tall, scaling a fence of equal height would be a challenge.

Unless he had help.

Knoop carefully inspected the fence and found several marks in the white paint that could have been made by a ladder. He checked the entire fence twice, and there were no other markings.

Beside the fence a path led to the lake. Knoop followed it to the sand where people were swimming and picnicking. A few rowboats and sailboats floated on the lake.

He followed the rear of the fence and took the other path back to the house. Then he returned to the sand and imagined the area at night. After dark, it would be nearly impossible to detect someone walking along the sand and stopping at the judge's fence.

But would he be carrying a ladder?

That was a ridiculous notion.

Unless . . .

As he had done with the other victims, Stuyvesant stalked the judge and learned his habits and his home.

So he knew ahead of time he would require a ladder.

Or?

Knoop spotted a long piece of driftwood in a bush at the edge of the sand. He lifted the wood. It stood about six feet tall and had several thick branches on it. He dragged the wood to the fence where the marks were and leaned the wood against the fence.

It was a perfect match.

After some trial and error, Knoop managed to scale the wood and fence and land with a thud onto the soft grass on the other side.

Then he entered the house through the French doors and found Matsell and Wagner in the living room.

"I found how he gained entrance," Knoop said.

Matsell and Wagner followed Knoop outside the house to the rear of the fence.

"The only part of the fence with scratches in the paint and the log fit perfectly," Knoop said.

"So he enters the house, shoots the judge, and exits the same way," Wagner said.

"Was any of the backyard furniture disturbed?" Knoop asked.

"I don't know," Wagner said.

"Let's check," Knoop said.

They returned to the backyard, where Knoop carefully inspected the chairs at the patio table and benches.

"Ask the housekeeper if any chairs or benches were moved," Knoop said. "We'll be in town for at least another day. And could you provide us a list of hotels and inns?"

"My letter of recommendation to Congress," Parker said.

Parker, Murphy, and Kai were on the porch, where Kai served coffee.

"How long do I have to decide?" Murphy asked.

"For this run, four months," Parker said.

Murphy looked at Kai.

"Kai?" he said.

"I have no objection, if that's what you're asking," Kai said.

"To be fair, Kai, I offered Murphy a position as a full marshal, but he turned me down," Parker said. "Having him represent our district to Congress would be the next best thing."

"And a great deal safer," Kai said.

"I'll sleep on it," Murphy said.

After visiting eleven hotels and inns without any luck, Matsell and Knoop retired to their own hotel. There Matsell showed Stuyvesant's photo to the clerk.

The clerk said, "I remember him. He stayed with us for about a week."

"When did he check out?" Matsell asked.

The clerk read his registry book. "Five nights ago," he said.

Knoop and Matsell entered the hotel dining room and found a table.

"Stuyvesant is proving to be quite resourceful," Matsell said.

"We need to return to New York and locate the other five jury members," Knoop said.

"Twelve jury members and a judge," Matsell said. "Thirteen. A baker's dozen."

CHAPTER TWELVE

"We should be back in around three weeks," Kai told Mrs. Leary. "We made arrangements with the general store to hold our furniture at their warehouse if it arrives early."

"Your things in the room?" Mrs. Leary said.

"We're leaving our luggage in the room," Kai said. "We'll have enough to bring back with us when we return."

"Don't worry about a thing, and have a safe trip," Mrs. Leary said.

They hugged, and then Kai left the boarding house and met Murphy, who was waiting for her on the porch.

"Did you send your telegram?" Kai asked.

"I did," Murphy said.

William Burke, seated at his desk in the White House, read the telegram the telegraph operator brought him.

He read it twice, then stood up and left his office. He walked through a maze of hallways, up a flight of stairs, then through another maze of hallways, and then knocked on the door to the Oval Office.

Burke opened the door and stepped inside. President Arthur sat behind his desk, reading legislature.

"Telegram from Murphy," Burke said.

"About?" Arthur asked.

"He's thinking of running for Congress again and wants to know if he has your support," Burke said.

"Congress?" Arthur said. "I thought he was still in New York assisting the police."

"He identified the killer and then returned to Fort Smith," Burke said. "Melvin Knoop is still helping with the investigation."

"Melvin . . . hogwash," Arthur said. "Tell Murphy to get back to New York before the stock market crashes and we have another panic of 1873."

"Tell Murphy?" Burke said.

"All right, ask him," Arthur said.

Knoop watched the scenery roll by outside his window from a riding car on the train. Matsell sat opposite him and kept busy with a newspaper.

"There are five members left from the jury," Knoop said.

Matsell looked up from the newspaper.

"What's on your mind, Melvin?"

"How do we locate them if they've left the city?"

"I don't know."

"I'll send Murphy a telegram and ask if he has any suggestions."

"That couldn't hurt," Matsell said.

Murphy's parents, Michael and Aideen, had supper ready when Murphy and Kai arrived at their farmhouse just before seven o'clock.

In his late sixties, Michael was still hardy and fit and often toiled twelve hours a day with his workers.

Aideen, a few years younger than her husband, possessed all the fire and vigor of her youth and she, not Michael, was the person in charge of the family.

Aideen greeted Kai with a hug and kiss while Michael and Murphy exchanged handshakes.

"You can tell us about your trip over supper," Michael said.

After supper, Murphy and Michael took coffee on the porch. Both men stuffed and lit their pipes. Michael added an ounce of his whiskey to their coffee.

"I've been thinking about another run for Congress," Murphy said. "In Fort Smith. Our house is nearly ready, and Kai will start teaching school on the reservation. Besides, it's always bothered me, the way I quit during my term."

"As I recall, President Garfield recruited you back into the Secret Service; I would hardly call that quitting," Michael said.

"Whatever the reason, I didn't finish my term," Murphy said. "I'd like to try it again and see it out."

"If that's what you want to do, I'll stand behind you," Michael said. "You have a good foreman and crew at the farm, a decent income from the whiskey crop, a wife who loves you, and you're still young enough to make your mark in government. Hell, your mother and Kai would worry a great deal less if they knew you were no longer chasing outlaws halfway across the plains."

"I expect that's true enough," Murphy said.

"It's getting late, son," Michael said. "Best you and Kai stay the night, and I'll take you over by buggy in the morning."

After washing and stacking the dirty cookware, Kai and Aideen took tea in Aideen's sitting room.

"Your son is considering running for Congress again," Kai said. "I expect he and Michael are discussing that very thing right now."

Aideen looked at Kai. "I see you're not entirely happy about the idea," she said.

"I'd much prefer him running around the halls of Congress than out on the prairie after some outlaw," Kai said.

Aideen nodded. "But?"

"I . . . I led him along, I'm afraid," Kai said. "I planted the seed and allowed him to think it was his idea. I've feeling a bit . . . guilty."

Aideen smiled. "I'm afraid you don't know my son as well as you think you do," she said. "If my son doesn't want to do something, nothing in heaven or on earth can move him. Just as when he wants to do something, nothing can stop him. Maybe you fed him the seed, but if he didn't want it, he would just spit it out."

"Did you ever . . . ?" Kai said.

"Manipulate Michael?" Aideen said. "After fifty years of marriage, Michael still swears it was his idea to propose."

Kai looked at Aideen.

"The secret to a happy marriage is to create the illusion that your man is in charge, even though they know that isn't true," Aideen said. "In the case of my son, he will never do what he doesn't want to do, so don't feel guilty about giving him a push in the direction you want him to go. If he doesn't want to go that way, you might as well be pushing a rock uphill against the Smoky Mountains."

Alone in the townhouse, Knoop sat at the desk in the study and composed a telegram he would send to Murphy in the morning.

Once he finished, he read it several times and made a few changes to the wording until he was satisfied.

Exhausted from traveling and making notes, Knoop turned in and fell asleep almost immediately.

CHAPTER THIRTEEN

"I'm afraid the Murphys have gone to their home in Tennessee," Mrs. Leary told the telegraph messenger. "Wait a moment, and I'll write down where you can send the telegram."

Murphy and Kai went for a ride after breakfast. Murphy rode his massive horse, Boyle, while Kai rode her smaller, more delicate pinto.

They rode west for about an hour and dismounted at the stream that divided Murphy's property from his father's. The stream traveled directly through his father's property and provided the fresh water for making whiskey.

They dismounted and sat in the shade of a tree beside the stream.

Boyle and the pinto nibbled grass.

Murphy stuffed and lit his pipe.

Kai looked at the stream.

"This is a world away from New York City," she said. "Or Washington."

"I haven't said I'm running for Congress yet," Murphy said.

"The thing of it is . . ." Kai said and paused.

"What?"

"Nothing. If you do this and win, how much time will you need to spend in Washington?"

"The average is around four months a year," Murphy said. "The rest of the time is spent in your home office, which would be in Fort Smith."

"That's not so bad, eight months at home," Kai said.

"If I run and if I win," Murphy said. "But that's not what I'm thinking about right now."

Kai looked at the stream and then stood up and began to unbutton her blouse. "Last one in has to cook dinner and wash the dishes," she said.

"I have a dozen detectives pouring over records trying to find the remaining jury members," Matsell said.

Mayor Edson slammed a copy of the *Post* onto his desk. "The judge who tried the case," he said. "He killed the judge who tried the blasted case. As of thirty minutes ago, the stock market was reaching panic status, so don't tell me your detectives are pouring over records. I want this murderer found sooner, not later, or you'll be retiring earlier than you expected."

"I understand, Mr. Mayor, but—"

"No buts. Just get the job done," Edson said.

At police headquarters, Knoop and the team of detectives sat at desks and read files and records containing all information on the jury members.

"Report," Matsell said when he entered the detective's squad room.

All the detectives were silent.

"Knoop, my office," Matsell said.

Knoop followed Matsell through a doorway, into the hall, and up two flights to Matsell's private office.

"The mayor is fit to be tied," Matsell said as he sat in the chair behind his desk.

"Commissioner, if I may suggest something," Knoop said.

"Suggest," Matsell said.

"We speak to friends, relatives, past employers, anybody who ever knew them until we locate where they are now," Knoop said.

"That's what my detectives have been doing without results," Matsell said.

"If Stuyvesant found them, so can we," Knoop said.

"That's the question, isn't it? How?" Matsell said.

Knoop sighed. "I sent a wire to Murphy asking him to return to New York," he said.

"Lord knows, we can use all the help we can get," Matsell said. "Has he replied yet?"

"I'd have to go home to check," Knoop said.

Matsell looked at Knoop.

After several seconds, Knoop said, "Oh, right," and stood up.

After dismounting at the corral, Kai went to the house while Murphy took care of Boyle and the pinto.

As Murphy walked to the porch, Kai stood there with an envelope in hand.

"A telegram," she said. "It was tucked into the screen door. Can you wait a few minutes to open it? I'll fix a pot of coffee."

Murphy sat and smoked his pipe until Kai came out with a tray holding a coffee pot and two cups. She poured and sat next to Murphy.

Murphy used his tiny penknife to slice open the envelope and then removed the telegram.

"It's from Knoop," he said.

"What does he say?"

"He says he needs my help in New York and if I can see my way clear to help him, he would forever be grateful," Murphy said.

"Grateful?" Kai said. "If you can see your way clear? He sounds desperate."

"The judge was killed," Murphy said. "Murdering a federally

appointed judge isn't taken lightly."

"I'll pack for both of us," Kai said.

"You don't have to go," Murphy said.

"I know," Kai said. "But I have an idea of my own."

Murphy looked at Kai.

"When was the last time your parents were away from home?" Kai said.

"Take my parents to New York City?" Murphy said.

"Why not?" Kai said. "When was the last time they traveled outside of Tennessee? We could see the sights while you and Melvin work. It might do them some good, you know."

"Let's have dinner with my parents tonight," Murphy said.

Knoop drank tea in the study as he poured over his pages of notes. The remaining five members of the jury had moved from the addresses they'd listed at the time of Stuyvesant's trial. To where, was the question.

He went back to the beginning and read his notes again.

The five missing jury members all moved from their listed residences between the end of the trial and present day.

They all lived in apartment buildings scattered throughout Manhattan. Thirteen years ago.

Where were they now?

Interviews with neighbors in the five apartment buildings proved fruitless. Tenant turnover was high, and most of the tenants had lived in the buildings less than three years.

Building records showed that the five jury members moved out between 1874 and 1879. Forwarding addresses were not left for the purpose of sending along mail.

Knoop's best guess was that the five remaining jury members had left the city.

But to where?

Matsell said, "If Stuyvesant found them, so can we."

The question in Knoop's mind was: how did Stuyvesant find them?

"No disrespect to our women, but why in the hell would I want to go to New York City?" Michael Murphy said.

They sat on the front porch of Michael and Aideen's farmhouse. Kai and Aideen held glasses of lemonade. Murphy and his father held cups of coffee and smoked their pipes.

"It was my idea, Michael," Kai said. "While your son is assisting the police with their investigation, I thought we could tour the city and take in the sights and the museums and such."

"I've been there once before, in forty-eight," Michael said. "I studied distilling at this brewery in Manhattan in a place called the Five Points. I can't say I enjoyed it much."

"More than thirty years ago, Michael," Aideen said. "I'm sure things aren't the same."

"We're leaving in the morning," Murphy said. "We'd really like you to go with us."

Aideen looked at Michael. "Michael?"

Michael sighed.

Aideen looked at Murphy. "That means yes."

Knoop tossed and turned, unable to sleep. His mind was a storm of thoughts and ideas, and none of them gave him relief.

What was he missing?

Where was the piece of the puzzle Stuyvesant had found that escaped him?

If Murphy didn't respond, Knoop was going to wire Pinkerton and request additional help.

Knoop gave up trying to sleep and returned to the study where, by lantern light, he poured over his notes again.

He woke up in the morning on the sofa when early sunlight filtered in through a window and struck him in the face.

He stood, stretched, and on his way to the kitchen, he paused when he noticed the telegram on the floor just under the mail slot in the door.

CHAPTER FOURTEEN

"Murphy will arrive around seven tonight," Knoop told Matsell when Matsell arrived in his carriage.

"Let's see if we can make some progress before he gets here," Matsell said.

"How handsome you look in a suit, Michael," Aideen said. "The last time you wore that suit was for a funeral, I believe."

"I don't see why I have to get dressed up like an organ grinder's monkey to ride a train," Michael said.

Kai grinned at Murphy.

"The train will be here any minute, Michael. Try to relax," Aideen said.

"Dad, let's get a newspaper for the ride," Murphy said.

"Go on," Michael said. "I'm going to smoke my pipe." He looked at Aideen. "It relaxes me."

Matsell addressed his squad of detectives and Knoop after lunch.

"I have a meeting with the mayor at four o'clock this afternoon," he said. "He's going to want a progress report and updates. Do we have any to give him?"

The squad of detectives and Knoop were silent.

"Then I suggest we all get back to work," Matsell said.

Matsell was surprised to see William Burke in Edson's office when he arrived for the meeting.

"Commissioner, you remember Mr. Burke?" Edson said.

"Yes, of course," Matsell said.

"The president has taken more than a passing interest in your investigation, Commissioner," Burke said. "And he is very concerned about the effect it is having upon the stock market. He doesn't want another panic such as what happened in 1873. A bad recession at this time could cost him reelection. A bad recession can set the country back to the days after the war, when men were out of work for years. In short, this man Stuyvesant needs to be captured, and damn quick."

"All that is understood, and we are doing all that we can to locate him," Matsell said.

"It's not enough, but that's not why I'm here right now," Burke said. "I'm meeting Murphy later on tonight. He's agreed to return and assist you in the matter. By assist, I expect him to take full command and with no resistance from you. Is that understood, Commissioner?"

Matsell looked at Edson.

"It's not a reflection on you, George," Edson said. "This comes from the president."

"Understood," Matsell said.

"Good. That's all, unless you have some progress to report?" Burke said.

"Not at this time," Matsell said.

"I have a question," Edson said. "Do you have any idea how Stuyvesant was able to locate the whereabouts of the jury members and the judge?"

"Off the list of jury members' applications provided by a court officer," Matsell said. "That officer is presently in Sing Sing awaiting trial."

"The judge's address in New Hampshire wasn't on those documents, was it?" Burke said.

"No, no it wasn't," Matsell said.

Edson nodded. "Go back to work, Commissioner," he said. "Make some progress."

Murphy stepped off the train, took Kai's hand, and guided her to the platform. Then he took Aideen's hand and she stepped down and stood next to Murphy.

Michael got down on his own power and said, "I hope we're walking after such a long ride."

"Afraid not," Murphy said.

At the end of the long platform, Burke and Knoop stood beside two carriages.

Murphy, Burke, and Knoop rode in one carriage, while Kai, Aideen, and Michael rode in a separate carriage directly behind them.

"I'm afraid there's been little progress on the judge's murder," Knoop said. "Mostly we are stumped as to how Stuyvesant knew where the judge had moved to after he retired."

"What about the remaining five jury members?" Murphy asked.

Knoop shook his head.

"As you can imagine, the president is quite upset about the situation," Burke said.

"Well then, the president can get off his ass and come to New York and help us," Murphy said.

"What is that God-awful smell?" Michael said.

"Horse dung, coal, and the East River," Kai said. "Early morning and later at night, it's not so bad."

"There are a lot of hours between early morning and later at night," Michael said.

"Michael, we'll be in the country tomorrow," Aideen said.

"You can endure a little smell for one night."

"Maybe so, but one thing I'd like to see is the telephone," Michael said.

"The telephone?" Aideen said.

"A city this big must have some," Michael said.

"I'll ask Mr. Burke," Kai said. "I'm sure he knows."

Michael stood on the sidewalk in front of the townhouse, looked up, shook his head, and said, "Ho-ley Shi—"

"Michael," Aideen snapped.

"Kai, why don't you and Knoop show the Murphys the house while your husband and I pick up our dinner from Delmonico's," Burke said.

"What does he mean 'pick up'?" Michael said.

Kai took Michael's arm and led him to the door. "I'll explain when I show you the house," she said.

"If this was happening out west, it would hardly get a mention," Burke said as he and Murphy rode to Delmonico's. "It would just be fodder for another dime-store novel. But New York City is the backbone of this country. Never mind the fact the judicial system itself is in jeopardy. People will refuse to serve on a jury if they fear for their lives. Qualified judges won't serve. The president is—"

"The president is feeling the heat," Murphy said.

Burke looked at Murphy.

"Yes," Burke said.

"What are we having for dinner?" Murphy said.

"I stopped by Delmonico's before I picked you up and ordered steaks and baked chicken and two types of pie for dessert," Burke said.

"My father loves pie," Murphy said.

"Sarcasm aside, Murphy, find this man and bring him to

114

justice," Burke said.

"I want something in return for my time," Murphy said.

Burke looked at Murphy and said, "How much? Name it."

"Not money, although I will ask for expenses."

"Then what?"

"Two things," Murphy said. "If I do file Congressional papers, I want the president's endorsement."

"I don't see how he can refuse," Burke said.

"The second is to appoint Knoop to the Secret Service," Murphy said.

"You're joking!"

"I'm not."

"I like Melvin, I do, but he couldn't guard a cat from a mouse," Burke said.

"Not for fieldwork. For his knowledge in forensics and investigative skills," Murphy said. "What he is doing at Pinkerton's is years ahead of what the police are doing, locally and federally. Pinkerton will then sell his technology to the government for a profit. Knoop winds up with nothing for his dedication and work at Pinkerton's. Let Knoop work for us directly, and the hell with Pinkerton."

"I see your point and it's valid," Burke said. "But Knoop isn't a citizen."

"Make him one," Murphy said. "How hard could that be?"

Burke sighed. "What kind of pie does your father like?"

After dinner, Murphy, Burke, Knoop, and Michael took coffee in the study of the townhouse.

"This is a fine big house," Michael said. "Kai said it was built for just one family."

"It's called a townhouse and is generally owned by one wealthy family," Burke said.

"Dad, why don't you sweeten our coffee?" Murphy said.

Michael produced a flask of his bourbon whiskey from a pocket and added some to the coffee cups.

"Tomorrow, while your mother and I and Kai visit with General Grant, what will you be doing, son?" Michael said.

"I won't know until I do it," Murphy said.

CHAPTER FIFTEEN

Kai kissed Murphy lightly on the lips and then said, "I'm not sure what time we will be back. After eight, I assume."

Murphy helped Kai into the carriage, where she sat next to Aideen.

"Keep my father in line," Murphy said.

"What does that—?" Michael said as the driver moved the carriage forward.

Knoop, standing next to Murphy, said, "What now?"

Murphy looked at his pocket watch. "What time will Matsell be here?"

"Eight, so he said."

"Where is Burke?"

"I saw him in the kitchen having coffee."

"I'll wait for Matsell," Murphy said. "Go in and get a fresh pot of coffee ready."

As they drank coffee in the study, Murphy said, "What is the largest newspaper in the city?"

"The *New York World* and the *New York Daily Times,*" Matsell said. "Why?"

"Which is the more accessible?" Murphy said.

"The *World* is owned by Jay Gould, and he keeps an office at the paper," Matsell said.

"That's where we will go first," Murphy said. "Burke, you're invited to go with us."

Jay Gould, one of the richest men in America, was also one of the most hated. Having made his fortune investing in railroads, he purchased the *New York World* for the opportunity to enter the court of public opinion.

"How is that court jester who occupies the White House?" Gould said to Burke once Burke, Murphy, Knoop, and Matsell were seated in his office.

Before Burke could respond, Murphy said, "How high up are we, Mr. Gould?"

"What?" Gould said.

"I counted twelve floors at about ten feet per floor," Murphy said. "That's about one hundred and twenty feet."

"I don't see what that has to—" Gould said.

"Disrespect the office of the presidency again and I will throw you out your office window. All your millions won't mean a damned thing when your feckless ass hits the pavement," Murphy said.

Shocked into silence for a few moments, Gould finally looked at Matsell. "Are you going to allow him to threaten me like this?" he said.

"I'm sorry, Mr. Gould. I wasn't paying attention," Matsell said.

"Mr. Murphy is a high-ranking member of the U.S. Secret Service, and he gets a mite testy when the presidency isn't respected," Burke said.

"Well, what is it you want?" Gould said.

"Access to your archives," Murphy said.

Gould sighed. "I'll bring you to see my editor."

As they followed the editor to the basement warehouse, Burke, walking beside Murphy, said, "Feckless?"

Murphy shrugged.

The editor opened the warehouse door and said, "Now exactly what are you looking for?"

"Is there any light in here?" Murphy said.

"This," the editor said and flicked several wall switches, "is the only room in the entire building with electric lighting."

Dozens of overhead light bulbs lit up at once, flooding the large warehouse with light.

"Mr. Gould felt that, with the amount of stored paper in a closed area, it would be best to use electric lighting over oil lamps," the editor said.

"Five years ago, Judge Carey retired from Superior Court," Murphy said. "I want to see the story covering his retirement."

"Five years ago, you say?" the editor said.

The editor carried a newspaper to the reading desk against the wall. "You can leave it on the desk when you are finished," he said. "And please turn off the lights when you are through."

"Melvin, read the story aloud," Murphy said.

Knoop read. When he reached the fifth paragraph, after four paragraphs of glowing accolades, Knoop said, "Judge Carey plans to retire to his summer home on Lake Winnipesaukee in New Hampshire. For many years, the judge has—"

"That's enough, Melvin," Murphy said. "We have our answer."

"When are you returning to Washington?" Murphy asked Burke as they arrived back at the townhouse.

"Ten a.m. train tomorrow," Burke said.

"Later this afternoon, do you feel like a ride uptown?" Murphy said.

"To where?" Burke said.

"Melvin, what do you feel like having for lunch?" Murphy said.

"Anything," Knoop said.

"Commissioner, do you know any good restaurants on the Upper West Side?" Murphy said.

"I know a great Italian restaurant on 114th Street," Matsell said.

"Italian good for you, Melvin?" Murphy said.

"In Chicago the street vendors sell what they call pizza," Knoop said. "I wonder if they have it here."

"I guess we'll find out," Murphy said.

In the carriage after leaving the Italian restaurant, Matsell said, "Ghastly stuff, that pizza pie."

"I tend to agree, and I doubt it will ever catch on with the American public," Burke said. "Now, Murphy, if you would kindly tell us where we are going."

Katherine Finch looked at Murphy with the frightened eyes of a doe being stalked by a cougar.

"I've already told you all I know," Katherine said. "Why do you keep harassing me?"

They were in the kitchen. Murphy and Katherine were the only two seated at the table. Burke, Knoop, and Matsell stood in the background.

"Where are your husband and the boy?" Murphy said.

"They are at the park playing in a baseball game," Katherine said.

"Do me a favor and place both hands on the table, palms up," Murphy said.

"Why?"

"Mrs. Finch, it may have sounded like a request, but it wasn't," Murphy said.

A lantern on the desk was on low flame. Matsell was asleep on the sofa against the wall. Knoop set the flame on the lantern to high and then woke Matsell by saying, "Commissioner, it's Melvin. I have some news."

Matsell opened his eyes and sat up. "What is it, Melvin?"

"From Sacramento," Knoop said and handed Matsell the telegram.

"Better notify Murphy in the morning," Matsell said. "Then go home and get some sleep."

A string of horse-drawn taxi carriages lined the platform of the railroad station in Columbus, Ohio, at one in the morning when the train arrived.

Murphy and Burke took a taxi to their hotel in the center of the city.

"How far to the prison?" Burke asked.

"Not far. An hour by carriage," Murphy said.

"So we don't need to get up at the crack of dawn?" Burke said.

Murphy grinned. "No."

Knoop had barely opened his eyes when he heard a knock on the front door. Armed with a cup of tea and wearing his long nightshirt, he went to see who it was.

Before Knoop reached the door, an envelope dropped through the mail slot. He picked it up, opened the envelope, and read the telegram from Kai, informing him that she and Murphy's parents would be returning around seven o'clock tonight.

Knoop sighed and then went to get dressed.

When Burke left his room at nine in the morning and went to the hotel dining room, Murphy was already at a table with a cup of coffee.

"Don't you ever sleep?" Burke said.

"Have some coffee. You'll feel better," Murphy said.

A waiter came to the table.

"Coffee, please," Burke said.

"I'll have five fried eggs with six strips of bacon, toast with butter and potatoes, and a small pot of coffee," Murphy told the waiter.

"Two poached eggs with toast for me," Burke added.

After the waiter left, Murphy said, "I arranged for a carriage. I figured you really didn't want to ride a horse for ten miles each way."

"I don't want to ride a horse for ten feet, much less ten miles," Burke said.

"A quiet ride in the country will give us time to discuss my campaign," Murphy said.

The waiter returned with a coffee for Burke and a small pot.

"How much do you think it will cost to finance my campaign?" Murphy said.

"Maybe thirty thousand to do it right," Burke said.

"Do you think I can raise that much?" Murphy said.

"I think you should be prepared to spend some of your own money," Burke said.

"How much of my own money?"

Burke took a sip of his coffee. "About thirty thousand."

Murphy grinned and picked up his coffee cup.

Before entering the Ohio Penitentiary, Murphy checked his .38 caliber short-nosed revolver with the guards at the front gates.

Warden Frank Bream sat behind his desk when Burke and Murphy were ushered into his office by a guard.

"After I received your telegram, I pulled the file on John Stuyvesant and studied up on the man," Bream said. "So I'm a bit confused as to why an assistant to the president and a secret service agent are interested in a common criminal like Stuyvesant."

"Since his release, Stuyvesant has murdered eight people in cold blood," Murphy said.

Bream stared at Murphy for several long seconds and then said, "The killings in New York City?"

"Does that answer your question?" Murphy said.

"My God," Bream said.

"Anything you can tell us about Stuyvesant would be helpful," Murphy said.

Bream picked up a file on his desk and opened it. "He was a model prisoner during his twelve years with us," he said. "He had a few friends, but mostly kept to himself. He spent a great deal of his free time in the library. The last few years he became very interested in government."

"Government?" Burke said.

Bream glanced at the file. "He even requested books on patents and real estate," he said. "He wrote a lot of letters to various agencies in Washington. I assumed it was just the man trying to better himself for when he was released."

"What agencies?" Murphy said.

Bream stood up. "We'll need to see the trusties."

The library was a large room in the south wing of the prison. There were twelve reading tables and shelves of books against every wall. Prisoners sat reading books or writing letters.

The library trusties were men serving life sentences for murder. One was named Crow, the other was Keef. Both men were in their sixties.

"Old John wrote ten, sometimes twelve letters a week," Crow said.

"Mostly to agencies in Washington," Keef said. "The patent

office, the justice department, the Recorder of Deeds, the bar association, things like that."

"We figured he wanted to better himself," Crow said.

"He was a pretty smart fellow," Keef said. "Never any trouble. He said he wanted to learn all the things he never had the opportunity to learn on the outside."

"He made friends with this lawyer fellow what murdered his wife," Crow said. "He got him started being interested in things."

"Is the lawyer still in prison?" Murphy said.

"Died about a year ago from the fever," Keef said.

"Did Stuyvesant ever talk about home? What he would do when he got out?" Murphy said.

"Once in a while," Crow said. "Not often."

"Right before he was released, he said he wanted to visit his sister and his son," Keef said. "Said he wanted to make things right. That's about it."

"All his letters and things?" Murphy said.

"Took them with him, as far as we know," Keef said.

As they walked to the front gate, Bream said, "I met with Stuyvesant the day before he was released, as I do with all prisoners upon their release. He seemed happy to be going home and showed no signs of doing what you say he did."

"Thank you for your time, warden," Murphy said.

"I'm sorry if your trip here was wasted," Bream said.

"The son of a bitch was plotting his revenge the whole time he was in prison and using the government to help him," Burke said.

"The government put him there. Who better to help him?" Murphy said.

"The bar association," Burke said. "How easy is that to find a particular lawyer?"

"Too easy."

Murphy stopped the carriage at the hotel and turned the reins over to a waiting groom.

Murphy and Burke entered the hotel where a desk clerk handed Murphy a telegram from Knoop. He read it and gave it to Burke.

"Far too easy," Murphy said.

CHAPTER SEVENTEEN

"Absolutely not," Burke said. "There is no way on earth I am going with you to Sacramento. I am returning to Washington first thing in the morning."

"I was hoping you would go to New York and escort Kai back to Fort Smith," Murphy said.

"She's with your parents."

"In Fort Smith, I'd like you to meet with Judge Parker about my campaign," Murphy said. "He's agreed to endorse me, and he's a powerful ally to have on our side."

"Our?" Burke said.

"And maybe you can smooth things over with Kai when you tell her I've decided to run," Murphy said.

They were in the hotel bar. Each held a glass of bourbon.

Burke looked at Murphy, and slowly he smiled.

"You afraid of Kai, aren't you?" Burke said.

"I didn't say that," Murphy said.

"Then tell her yourself."

"Would you just do this for me?" Murphy said. "I have to go to Sacramento."

"I would have never thought it possible that you'd be afraid of anything." Burke grinned. "Scared of your own wife."

"Are you going to do it or not?"

"Hell, yes, just to see her reaction." Burke gloated.

Knoop peered through the curtains in the living room as he

132

waited for Kai's carriage to arrive.

A few minutes before five in the afternoon, the carriage pulled to the curb, and he rushed outside to greet Kai and Murphy's parents.

"How was your trip?" Knoop said as he helped Kai down from the carriage.

"Wonderful," Kai said. "The general and Michael got along like old friends. Where is Murphy?"

Knoop looked at Kai, and she instantly knew something was wrong.

"Melvin, where is my husband?" she said.

"I'm not sure," Knoop said. "With Mr. Burke. They went to Ohio."

"Ohio? What for?" Michael said as he helped Aideen down from the carriage.

"For . . . it's a very long story," Knoop said. "We'll talk in the house."

"California?" Kai said as she glared at Knoop.

"I'm not sure, but it's possible," Knoop said. "Mr. Burke will be here sometime tomorrow and explain everything."

Michael looked at Kai and said, "Now, Kai, before you're too hard on him, my son does have a job to do."

"Yes, here in New York, not three thousand miles away," Kai said. She scowled at Knoop. "And you were supposed to watch him."

Kai stormed out of the living room, went upstairs to her bedroom, and slammed the door.

Knoop looked at Aideen. "I did watch him," he said. "I'm just not crazy enough to try to stop him."

"She's not mad at you, Melvin," Aideen said. "She's not even mad at my son, not really. Mostly she's mad at herself."

"Herself? Why?" Knoop said.

"I'm afraid you have to be a woman to understand that one," Aideen said.

Aideen left the room and went upstairs to Kai's bedroom.

"I don't know about you, Melvin, but I need a drink," Michael said.

"Make it a big one," Knoop said.

"Sorry to drop in on you so late, Melvin, but I've just left a meeting with the mayor and he thinks that, since Stuyvesant has left New York, we should downgrade our efforts."

"I'm not sure I understand," Knoop said.

They were in the study. It was after ten o'clock, and Melvin wore his long nightshirt, as he'd been ready for bed before Matsell arrived.

"Pour us a drink, would you, Melvin?" Matsell said. "I think we both could use one."

Knoop filled two small glasses with whiskey and gave one to Matsell.

"Thank you, Melvin," Matsell said.

"The mayor wants to end the search for Stuyvesant because we have been unable to locate the remaining five jury members?" Knoop said.

"He thinks, and I find it difficult to disagree with him, that the remaining jury members have left New York, and that to waste extreme resources at this time would be wasteful and fruitless," Matsell said.

Knoop sipped his drink and nodded. "Murphy won't quit," he said.

"No, no, I expect he won't," Matsell said. "But Murphy is a federal officer, and he can far exceed my limits. Yours, too."

Knoop nodded. "I really enjoyed working with you, Commissioner," he said.

"Same here, Melvin. I learned a great deal from you both,

and I will put it to good use," Matsell said.

"Thank you," Knoop said.

Matsell set his empty glass on the bar. "Good night, Melvin," he said.

Burke arrived at the New York City townhouse in time for breakfast. While Knoop was glad to see him, Kai was none too happy.

"Mr. Burke, just where in the hell is my husband?" she demanded before he even set down his suitcase.

"He should be arriving in Sacramento around noon today," Burke said.

Kai glared at Burke. "What is his business in Sacramento?"

"The prosecutor in the case we're investigating was murdered in Sacramento, and Murphy's looking into it," Burke said. "He asked me to go with you to Fort Smith, and he'll be home in five days."

"Five days?" Kai said.

"That's what he told me to tell you," Burke said.

"Breakfast is almost ready," Kai said.

In the dining room, Michael said, "Mr. Burke, I'm anxious to see a telephone. Would you know where I might find one in the city?"

"I suppose a day of sightseeing won't hurt anything," Kai said.

Burke was able to use his considerable influence to gain entrance to the telephone exchange in Lower Manhattan.

"There are less than one thousand telephones in New York City at the moment, and most of them are in the financial district and stock market," a guide explained. "However, it is estimated that by nineteen hundred, a third of the population will have at least one telephone per household. Many will have two."

"Why would you need two?" Michael said.

"If you live in a house with two floors, you might want one for each floor," the guide said.

"Well, how does it work?" Michael said.

The guide picked up the mouthpiece and handed it to Michael. "When I crank the handle, a voice will ask you what party you want. Ask for the time."

"The time?"

The guide nodded and cranked the handle. "Speak into the mouthpiece."

"Operator. How may I help you?" a female voice said into the receiver.

Astounded, Michael looked at Aideen.

"Ask for the time, dear," Aideen said.

"Can you tell me the time?" Michael said.

"Yes, sir. It's three minutes past noon."

"Thank you, sir," Michael said to the operator.

The guide took the receiver and hung it up.

"Thank you, sir," Burke said. "Now, who is for lunch?"

Murphy walked from the railroad station in Sacramento to the center of town. As the state capital of California, Sacramento was a bustling, political town of twenty thousand residents.

Carriages were everywhere. Women wore high fashion. Politics was in the air and on everyone's lips.

He found the sheriff's office on Main Street. It was a large brick building, two stories high. The deputies on duty on the first floor wore suits instead of uniforms. Murphy went to the front desk where a deputy was on duty.

"Murphy, US Secret Service here to see Sheriff Pruitt," Murphy said as he showed the deputy his identification.

"The sheriff is expecting you," the deputy said. "I'll have someone take you to his office."

In his mid-fifties and stout, Pruitt had a head full of graying hair. He was nearly a foot shorter than Murphy when he stood up behind his desk to shake hands.

"Terrible thing about that lawyer fellow," Pruitt said. "But your telegram didn't say why a federal officer was interested enough in him to travel clear across the country."

"Where is his house?" Murphy said.

"On the west side of town."

"I'll tell you about it on the way," Murphy said.

Thomas Griffin had purchased a two-story townhouse in a quiet neighborhood and converted the first floor into his law office. He and his wife of thirty years, Joan, occupied the eight rooms on the second floor.

"Unfortunately, Mrs. Griffin is hospitalized at the moment," Pruitt said as he used a key to unlock the door to Griffin's law office. "She discovered her husband's body after the gunshot awakened her at ten-thirty in the evening."

Murphy looked at the desk and chair. The back of the chair and the front of the desk were both covered in dried blood.

"He was shot in the head from the front," Murphy said. "I can tell by the blowback of the blood and the splatter on the desk. Did the medical examiner recover the .36 caliber ball?"

Pruitt looked at Murphy. "What was left of it."

"No footprints in the blood on the floor, so the killer stood back, probably ten feet, close to the door," Murphy said.

Pruitt looked at the floor.

"The door is completely intact, so the door was unlocked," Murphy said. "He walks in unannounced, fires one shot, turns, and leaves. The shot woke up his wife; did it wake up any neighbors?"

"This neighborhood is in bed before ten," Pruitt said. "The walls of this house are pretty solid. My people spoke to every neighbor on both sides of the block, and no one heard a thing."

Murphy peered at the bloodstained documents on the desk.

"He was practicing civil law," he said.

"What you said on the ride over. He was a prosecutor in New York," Pruitt said. "He was probably sick of criminals and decided to return home and take up civil law."

"How long had he been living here?" Murphy said.

"His wife said just over four years."

"Do you know where the local bar association is located?"

"Yes. A few blocks from the Capitol Building."

"I'd like to visit the bar association and then Mrs. Griffin at the hospital," Murphy said. "And how many hotels are there in town?"

"Hotels? Many. This is the state capital."

"I need one for myself, and we can check the other hotels when we have the chance."

"Check for what?"

"The man who murdered Thomas Griffin."

"You're the second person to inquire about Mr. Griffin in the past thirty days," the manager at the local bar association said.

"Who was the first, and what was the inquiry?" Murphy said.

"It came by telegram," the manager said. "Hold on a moment, and I'll get it."

Murphy and Pruitt waited while the manager went to a file cabinet and returned with a telegram. He handed it to Murphy.

I'm interested in locating an old friend of mine from New York City, Mr. Thomas Griffin, an attorney. I heard he relocated to Sacramento, and I would like to look him up. Signed, W. Carey.

"Who is W. Carey?" Pruitt said.

"The judge Stuyvesant murdered before he murdered Griffin," Murphy said.

"I'm sorry, but Mrs. Griffin is still heavily sedated and asleep," a doctor at the hospital said. "Maybe in a few days, when her children arrive from back east, you can see her."

"Thank you," Murphy said.

Murphy and Pruitt left the hospital and entered Pruitt's carriage.

"Let's check hotels," Murphy said.

"He was here," the desk clerk at the Sacramento Arms said. "He stayed two days and then paid his bill and left."

"Look again," Murphy said.

The desk clerk looked at the photograph of Stuyvesant.

"That's Mr. Carey, no doubt," the desk clerk said.

"Did he say where he might be going next when he checked out?"

"No, and I didn't ask. He did request a taxi to take him to the railroad station, though."

"Thank you. Now, I need a room for the night, and where is the nearest telegraph office?" Murphy said.

"We can send a telegram right from the hotel," the desk clerk said.

"Have someone come to my room in thirty minutes to pick it up," Murphy said. "Sheriff Pruitt, thank you for your time today."

"Where are you off to next?" Pruitt said.

"Home."

CHAPTER EIGHTEEN

"I wired Mrs. Leary and told her to hold three rooms at my boarding house," Kai said. "We should arrive in time for supper."

Knoop looked down the tracks and said, "The train is coming."

"I can't say for sure if I've seen this man, but he does look familiar," the ticket clerk at the Sacramento railroad station said.

"Look again," Murphy said.

The clerk took another look at the photograph.

"I see hundreds of people a day," the clerk said. "A thousand or more in a week. He looks familiar, but I can't be certain."

"Thanks," Murphy said. "I need to go to Fort Smith, so find me the quickest route."

"A sleeping car?"

"Unless you expect me to sleep standing up with the horses."

Knoop poured over his notes as he sipped coffee in the dining car. He was alone until Burke entered the car and joined him.

"How is it going, Melvin?" Burke asked.

"I'm giving myself a headache," Knoop said. "We know Stuyvesant used the jury list to find the jury members still living in New York, the newspaper to find the judge, and the bar association to find the lawyer, but I'm stumped as to how he will locate the remaining five jurors."

"Sometimes, when I'm dealing with a particular problem in Washington, I find it best to set it aside for a day or two and then tackle it with a new perspective," Burke said.

"Yes, you're right of course. It's just I can't help feeling I've missed some clue or piece of evidence that might help apprehend him," Knoop said.

"Close everything up, Melvin. There is something I wish to discuss with you," Burke said.

Knoop closed his files.

"Murphy requested this and, after pondering it for a bit, I agree with him," Burke said. "Murphy wishes you to join the Secret Service as a forensics investigator. I think he would like you to replace him in that capacity if he runs for Congress."

"But you have to be a citizen to become a Secret Service agent," Knoop said.

"That can be arranged very easily," Burke said. "And instead of Pinkerton taking credit for your work and selling it to the government, you will be directly involved with all new police tactics and advances."

"This was Murphy's idea?" Knoop said.

"Yes, and I have to say it's a damned good one," Burke said.

"I don't know what to say," Knoop said.

"Say yes," Burke said.

Murphy sat in a chair at the small desk in his sleeper car and reviewed his notes.

Stuyvesant was proving to be a highly intelligent individual and as committed as he was smart.

He obviously learned a great deal in prison and was using his working knowledge of the system to enact his revenge.

Finding the jury members still living in New York was a fairly easy task. Even finding the judge wasn't too difficult. Locating

141

Griffin by using the bar association showed a higher intelligence than a normal ex-convict.

Murphy filled a small water glass with whiskey from his flask, then stuffed and lit his pipe.

It wouldn't take long for the judge's murder and the murder of Griffin to make the front pages of every newspaper in the country.

Such news would further disrupt the stock market and cause an economic recession that could worsen if the remaining five jury members were murdered.

Murphy closed his notebook and thought about the situation for a moment. It occurred to him that Stuyvesant wasn't seeking revenge against the New York City judicial system that sent him to prison; he was out to damage the entire nation.

And he was off to a pretty good start.

"Mr. Burke, what brings you to my courthouse?" Judge Parker said when Burke was ushered into Parker's office by a deputy.

"Two things," Burke said. "My never-ending quest to find the perfect bourbon, and Murphy."

Parker stood from behind his desk and went to the bar against the wall. "Have an unopened bottle of Murphy's father's bourbon," he said. "In my experience, it's as close to perfect as there is."

Parker poured a few ounces into whiskey glasses and gave one to Burke.

"Well, that takes care of the first thing," Parker said. "Now, what about Murphy?"

"Apparently, I'm to be his campaign manager," Burke said.

"So he's serious then?" Parker said. "About Congress."

"Very."

"And Kai?"

"She'd rather have Murphy four months out of the year in

Washington, than out on the trail chasing outlaws," Burke said.

"I can't fault her for that," Parker said. "Where is he, by the way?"

"California, last I heard," Burke said. "He should be here inside a week or less."

"On that New York shooting?"

Burke nodded. "Oh, and by the way, I'm taking Kai and Murphy's parents to Delmonico's for dinner tonight. Join us. Seven o'clock."

Murphy was dozing in his riding car bunk when he opened his eyes and sat up. He grabbed his notebook and skimmed pages.

"What did he say?" Murphy said aloud. "Keef, the trustee."

He flipped a few more pages and stopped.

"The patent office, the justice department, the Recorder of Deeds, the bar association, things like that," Murphy read aloud.

Murphy closed the notebook.

"Of course," he said aloud.

"The last time I was in Fort Smith there was nothing but wood buildings and mud for sidewalks," Michael said.

"Michael, that was thirty or more years ago," Aideen said.

"All I'm saying is it's changed a great deal," Michael said.

"Mr. Murphy, I've been waiting for the opportunity to tell you that your whiskey is the finest I've ever tasted," Parker said.

"I'm flattered, Judge," Michael said. "If you will allow it, I shall send you a case when I return home."

"Seeing as how you reside outside of my jurisdiction and it can't be considered a bribe, I accept," Parker said.

Seated next to Parker, Burke softly cleared his throat.

Michael grinned. "And a case to you as well, Mr. Burke," he said.

"Now that Mr. Murphy has supplied you two with enough

whiskey to keep you drunk until Christmas, is there any news of my husband?" Kai said.

"He's in route," Burke said. "That's all I know at the moment."

Murphy found a conductor in a riding car.

"I need to change trains for Washington. Where is the closest stop?" Murphy said.

"Topeka," the conductor said. "From there it's a straight run into DC."

"Thank you," Murphy said.

He took a seat beside a window and smoked his pipe and worked out some details in his mind.

After returning to Kai's boarding house, Burke, Michael, Knoop, and Judge Parker took chairs on the porch and had a drink of Michael's bourbon.

"Mr. Burke, what are your plans concerning Murphy's run for Congress?" Parker said.

"We have four months until the primary," Burke said. "I haven't run a campaign in a while, but with a good speech writer and some favorable endorsements from you and the president, I'd say Murphy has a fair chance at winning the seat."

"Well, you can count on my endorsement and my full support," Parker said. "And now I must say good night. I have an early trial in the morning."

After Parker left, Knoop stood and said, "I'm going to turn in. It's been a long couple of days."

"Melvin, we need to go to Washington to start the process of getting his campaign off the ground," Burke said. "As soon as Murphy arrives, we'll head north."

Knoop nodded. "Good night, Mr. Burke, Mr. Murphy."

"He's a nice young fellow," Michael said after Knoop went inside.

"And very valuable to the government," Burke said.

"Another taste?" Michael said.

"Please."

Michael lifted the bottle off the deck and filled the glasses.

"About my son, do you really believe he wants to run for Congress again?" Michael said.

"I believe he wants to make Kai happy and provide her stability," Burke said.

"That's not the same thing," Michael said.

"No, no it isn't," Burke said. "But many men make considerations on behalf of their wives. It's just the nature of things."

"Mr. Burke, my son has been a great many things in his life," Michael said. "Some he's good at and some not so good. The only thing he's ever been exceptional at is what he's doing right now. Exceptional is hard to find in any profession."

Burke sipped whiskey and looked at Michael.

"Just something to ponder," Michael said.

CHAPTER NINETEEN

"It's a pleasure to have you aboard, Mr. Knoop," President Arthur said as he shook Knoop's hand.

"Thank you, Mr. President," Knoop said. "I will do my best never to let you down."

"William, this calls for a drink," Arthur said.

Burke went to the liquor cabinet, found a bottle of Michael's bourbon, filled three small glasses, and gave one to Arthur and Knoop.

"Gentlemen, to your health," Arthur said.

After three shots were downed, Burke said, "I'll find a suitable residence for Melvin and when Murphy arrives home, he can . . ."

"He's on his way here. Tonight," Arthur said.

"Are you sure?" Burke said.

Arthur picked up a telegram on his desk and handed it to Burke. "He sent this from Chicago two days ago."

Burke read the telegram quickly. "He doesn't say why he's coming to Washington instead of going home to Fort Smith."

"I'm sure, when Murphy arrives, he will tell us," Arthur said. "He should be here in time for dinner."

Burke and Knoop met Murphy at the station when the seven o'clock train arrived in Washington.

"The president is holding dinner for us," Burke said.

Murphy tossed his suitcase into the back of Burke's carriage.

146

"Good, I'm starved."

Once Murphy, Knoop, and Burke were aboard the carriage and the driver steered them toward the White House, Knoop said, "What did you find out in Sacramento?"

"It was Stuyvesant, no doubt," Murphy said.

"Did you wire Kai about stopping in Washington?" Burke said.

"I did, and imagine she's none too happy," Murphy said.

"All right, so why are you here?" Burke said.

"We'll talk over dinner," Murphy said. "I hope Arthur's chef doesn't skimp. I haven't eaten since breakfast."

"Nebraska beef, the best in the country," Arthur said as he sliced into a thick cut of steak.

Murphy, Burke, Knoop, and Arthur sat at the dining table in Arthur's private quarters in the White House.

"So, what did you learn in Sacramento that prompted a trip back to Washington?" Burke said.

Murphy sliced into his steak and placed the bite into his mouth. He chewed slowly and washed it down with a sip of water.

"Stuyvesant believed from the start that he was sentenced to prison unjustly," Murphy said. "His statement to the judge when sentenced bears that out. He didn't show remorse, but anger in the courtroom at the injustice of being found guilty when, as he put it, he was the one who was wronged."

"That's the entire reason behind his revenge, isn't it?" Arthur said. "But what does that have to do with you being here?"

"Stuyvesant is well above average in intelligence," Murphy said. "His military record testifies to that. Burke, do you remember what the trustee said to us when we visited the prison?"

"Yes," Burke said. "That Stuyvesant took an interest in the

147

government and wrote a great many letters."

"To the bar association, which is how he located Thomas Griffin," Murphy said. "And the Recorder of Deeds in Washington."

"Whatever for?" Arthur asked.

"Deeds are public knowledge," Murphy said. "If you need to locate someone who is a land or property owner, the Recorder of Deeds is a sure way to locate them."

Arthur, Burke, and Knoop stared at Murphy.

"He used his years in prison to learn the system of government in case he needed to locate the jury members who might have moved away from New York City," Burke said.

"He planned this for many years," Arthur said.

"It goes even deeper than that," Murphy said. "His revenge isn't just against the jury that sent him away; it's against the entire government he believes allowed his conviction to happen. He wants to cause a panic in the judicial system and the economy by causing a stock market recession, like in seventy-three."

"How can one man damage an entire country?" Arthur said.

"That could be asked of Napoleon and Nero," Burke said.

"What if . . . what if others copy what Stuyvesant has done?" Knoop said. "It's been in all the newspapers. Others who feel as he does might take it upon themselves to copy him."

"That would be catastrophic," Arthur said. "Who would want to sit on a jury, from New York City to the smallest western town, knowing they could be killed for doing their civic duty?"

Burke looked at Murphy. "Suggestions?"

"Melvin, have you been sworn in as yet?" Murphy said.

"This afternoon," Knoop said.

"Good. Mr. President, assign Melvin to head a task force of agents to contact the Recorder of Deeds in each state and check to see if our five missing jury members have purchased land or property. I suspect Stuyvesant has been doing this for months now."

"You're talking about a dozen counties by state and territory," Burke said.

"I know, but if Stuyvesant is doing this alone, an entire team should be able to do it faster and more efficiently," Murphy said.

Arthur nodded. "Well, Melvin, you have your first assignment," he said.

Knoop looked at Murphy. "Mr. Murphy?" he said meekly.

"In the morning, I'm going home," Murphy said. "Once you find the remaining five jury members, it's just a matter of sending teams of Secret Service agents to safeguard them until Stuyvesant is caught or killed."

Burke and Arthur exchanged quick glances and Arthur gave Burke a tiny, barely noticeable head nod.

After dark, Murphy and Burke sat on the rear porch of the White house and sipped coffee laced with bourbon.

"Did you file my papers?" Murphy asked.

"I did, yes."

"So what now?"

"Campaign season starts in a month," Burke said. "I'll set up a headquarters in Fort Smith in two weeks. Then we can get busy on strategy, newspaper and print ads, and, of course, stumping."

"My house should be ready by then. You can have a room for as long as you like," Murphy said.

"That would cut down on expenses," Burke said.

Murphy stuffed and lit his pipe.

Burke removed a cigar from his holder and lit it with a wood match.

Both men were silent for a few moments as they puffed.

Finally Burke sighed and said, "You can't just turn your back on the Stuyvesant case, Murphy. Think of your country for God's sake."

"I'm thinking of my wife, something I didn't do the first go-round," Murphy said.

"Dammit man, Kai will understand," Burke said. "She'll get mad, throw things, cuss me out, but in the end she will understand."

"I promised Kai," Murphy said. "I won't break that promise to her so Chester Arthur can win a second term. Knoop is more than capable of heading a team of agents to find those five missing jury members."

"Is he capable of hunting the man down and bringing him to justice?" Burke said. "Are any of the agents, for that matter? They are protectors of the president, not manhunters."

"There are dozens of US marshals capable of organizing a manhunt," Murphy said. "And the army, too, for that matter."

"I told the president you'd say that very thing," Burke said.

"Then he won't be disappointed, will he?" Murphy said.

"Do you really think your conscience will let you walk away from what you know deep down is your duty?" Burke said.

"My conscience would bother me a lot more if I broke my word to Kai," Murphy said. "Tell that to Chester Arthur."

"I will," Burke said.

"I expect to see you in Fort Smith in two weeks," Murphy said.

"I'll be there," Burke said.

"Would you like your coffee sweetened a bit more?" Murphy said.

"By all means," Burke said.

Kai sat in the rocking chair, alone on the porch of the boarding house, and sipped from a cup of tea.

Despite the fact that close to four thousand people lived in Fort Smith, after dark the town was quiet enough to hear the night frogs croaking their music.

She listened to their croaks and peepings from the yard.

The porch door opened, and Aideen stepped out with a cup of tea and sat beside Kai in the second rocker.

"It's too hot to sleep," Aideen said.

"It is," Kai agreed. "Thank you for staying to help with the furniture. We'll follow the freight company wagons right after breakfast."

Aideen sipped tea and looked at Kai. "I have been trying to get Michael to buy new furniture since before the war. He claims you don't throw out something that is still good just because it has a few miles on it. I'm hoping this might finally convince him it's time."

Kai grinned. "His son is just as stubborn," she said.

Aideen sipped more tea. "I know what you're thinking," she said. "That when the president sends Mr. Burke to ask my son to tackle the job no one else wants, he will go off and leave you."

"What do you think?" Kai said.

"I know my son," Aideen said. "He won't do anything unless you allow it."

Kai sipped some tea and stared into the darkness.

"Let's try to get some sleep," Aideen said.

CHAPTER TWENTY

Burke and Knoop escorted Murphy to the railroad station in Burke's carriage.

"I'll see you in two weeks," Murphy said to Burke.

"You will," Burke said.

"Melvin, good luck to you," Murphy said.

"Thank you for everything, Mr. Murphy," Knoop said.

Murphy boarded the train.

As the train left the station, Burke looked at Knoop.

"Is that a tear in your eye, Melvin?" Burke said.

"Maybe," Knoop said.

"Melvin, there is no crying in the Secret Service," Burke said.

Nine freighter haulers carried furniture into the house and set things down according to Kai's instructions.

By early afternoon, the three bedrooms, kitchen, parlor, living room, study, and sewing room were completely furnished.

"The child's room is beautiful," Aideen said. "And so is the entire house."

"Why are there two desks in the study?" Michael said.

"One is for me to correct test papers and prepare lessons for school," Kai said.

Michael sat on the sofa in the living room. "Very comfortable," he said. "Aideen, I think we could use some new things for our place. Brighten it up a bit. It seems we had the same belongings since before the war."

"Maybe Kai can show us the catalog in town that she ordered from?" Aideen said.

"That's a good idea," Michael said.

"I need to buy new linens, blankets, and towels anyway. We might as well go right now," Kai said.

"Aideen, why didn't you notice we needed some new furnishings?" Michael said.

"I just didn't notice, I guess," Aideen said.

"Michael, would you like to see the blueprints for the corral and barn?" Kai said.

"I would, actually," Michael said.

Murphy read the Washington newspaper on the ride south to Fort Smith. There were several stories about the "Ghost Shooter" and the effect he was having on the stock market and the drop in jury pools in major cities around the country.

Editors were calling for swift action to be taken by the police. Opinion pieces called on the president and the justice department to take action and end the "Ghost Shooter's" reign of terror.

The financial pages reported a severe drop in the stock market, including railroad and steel, resulting in heavy financial losses.

The president was not without a valid point. One or two more murders of jury members could throw the stock market and economy into a recession.

Murphy closed the newspaper and set it on the seat beside him. He took out his pipe and pouch and filled the bowl with tobacco. He struck a wood match, lit the pipe, and watched scenery roll by outside the window.

He'd paid more than his fair share to the government. He'd shed enough blood for ten lifetimes during the course of his duty to his country.

He'd endured enough pain, mental and physical, doing his duty to satisfy any man, presidents and generals included.

He had lost his first wife and child to the Civil War. A few years ago, he lost Sally Orr, a woman he loved. She'd been a casualty to an assignment from the president.

Murphy vowed he would not lose Kai over some insane killer's revenge.

Murphy stepped off the train at just after seven o'clock in the evening and walked to the center of Fort Smith.

The town was still bustling with the day's activity.

He walked straight to the boarding house and was surprised to see his parents and Kai on the front porch.

"Ma, Dad, I'd have thought you'd be home by now," Murphy said as he kissed Kai on the cheek.

"We wanted to take a look at your new house and we helped Kai with the furniture," Michael said.

"We plan to leave in the morning," Aideen said.

"Kai, want to go with them?" Murphy said. "I'd like to bring Boyle and your horse to Fort Smith."

"All right," Kai said. "Have you had your dinner yet?"

"No, and I'm starved," Murphy said.

"Let's all take a walk to Delmonico's for dinner," Kai said.

As she linked arms with Murphy, Kai leaned in close and whispered, "We'll talk about Sacramento later."

Knoop left the room he was staying in at the White House and went downstairs to the telegraph room.

Three operators were pouring over received telegrams.

"Any positive replies?" Knoop asked.

"Nothing yet, Mr. Knoop, but remember, the majority of telegrams went out late," an operator said. "Consider all the time zones and the necessary research involved."

"Yes, of course," Knoop said. "Well, good night, gentlemen."

As he walked back to his bedroom, Knoop noticed a light under the door to Burke's private office. He stopped and knocked on the door.

"Yes?" Burke said from inside the office.

Knoop opened the door and entered the office. Burke sat behind his desk, cigar in one hand, and drink in the other.

"Melvin, what are you doing wandering around at this hour?" Burke said.

"I couldn't sleep," Knoop said. "I thought I'd check the telegrams."

"And?"

"Nothing yet."

"Sit."

Knoop took a chair opposite the desk. Burke opened a drawer, produced a bottle of Michael's whiskey and a small glass, and poured Knoop a drink.

"To help you sleep," Burke said.

"Thank you," Knoop said as he lifted the glass and took a tiny sip.

"There is one thing you must learn when you serve the government, Melvin," Burke said. "Patience. The wheels of government turn very slowly, my friend. If you try to grease the wheels too much, they fall off the cart."

"I'm realizing that," Knoop said.

"There is something else," Burke said. "I see it in your eyes. What is it?"

"It's not for me to say, Mr. Burke," Knoop said.

"As a private citizen, I agree with you. As a Secret Service agent for the United States, speak your mind," Burke said.

Knoop took another sip of bourbon.

"I'm just disappointed that Mr. Murphy went home," Knoop said.

Burke puffed up a gray cloud of cigar smoke and said, "So am I, Melvin. But if anyone has earned the right to stay home with his wife, it is Murphy."

Knoop nodded.

"Finish your drink and then get some sleep," Burke said. "Tomorrow is a new day, and new days have a habit of bringing news."

As Kai brushed her hair in front of the dresser mirror, she glanced at Murphy, who was seated on the bed.

"You should have wired to let me know you were going to Washington before you decided to go," Kai said.

"It was spur of the moment, something that needed to be reported," Murphy said.

"And if you were injured or killed in Washington, and I was expecting you home from California?" Kai said. "Which you shouldn't have gone to in the first place."

"I wasn't injured or killed, and the chance presented itself unexpectedly," Murphy said.

Kai set her brush on the dresser, stood, and looked at Murphy.

"Here it is, Murphy," Kai said. "I will be a good wife to you, a very good wife, but I told you once before I can't and won't live with ghosts. I am very proud of the lawman you are, of the man you are, but even you can't be a lawman forever. The ghosts aren't just of your dead wife and child, or that other woman who died, but of the job you've done so well for so very long. It's time to choose what you want more: a wife and family or the service."

"You have a beautiful color when you're angry," Murphy said.

Kai sighed loudly. "Hopeless. You're hopeless."

She got into bed beside Murphy and lowered the lantern on

the bedside nightstand.

"No more spur of the moment adventures," she said.

"No?"

"No."

"Actually, I'm thinking of having a spur of the moment adventure right now," Murphy said.

Kai blew out the lantern.

"Hopeless," she said.

CHAPTER TWENTY-ONE

About an hour south of Fort Smith, Murphy and Michael went to the smoking car so they could smoke without disturbing other passengers in the riding car.

"Give him time to make the adjustment, Kai," Aideen said. "My son has been a man of action since the war. He'll need some time to settle in to a new routine of daily life that doesn't involve chasing outlaws halfway across the country."

"I know." Kai sighed. "I'm afraid I haven't been very patient with him about the whole thing."

"Tell me about your first husband," Aideen said.

"He was a US marshal, and he was killed serving warrants," Kai said. "He was a very kind man, probably too kind to be a lawman. It was right before the war. I was much younger then and probably a lot stronger. I don't think I would survive if I lost a second husband the same way as the first."

"You survived being kidnapped by the Sioux and the loss of a child," Aideen said. "You survived the loss of a husband and are worried about losing a second."

"Yes, I am," Kai said.

"I'm going to tell you something I've never even told my son," Aideen said. "My son was born a twin. His brother was much weaker and sick, and he died after three days. Michael buried the baby in the family cemetery in his mother's plot. It's unmarked about the baby. I've never spoken of it since. I just raised my son as best as I knew how."

Kai stared at Aideen.

"Men fight the wars and build the buildings and bridges, but women are far stronger when it comes to carrying a burden," Aideen said. "In that department, your shoulders are much broader than my son's."

Kai looked at Aideen and nodded.

Knoop and Burke waited in the White House telegraph room as operators sent and received messages.

"It's after noon, Melvin. Let's get some lunch," Burke said.

"I'm not really hungry," Knoop said.

"Then keep me company," Burke said. "An operator will bring us any news immediately."

Burke and Knoop went to the first floor where the cafeteria was located. Fresh roast beef sandwiches and beef stew were on the menu. Burke got a sandwich and a cold glass of milk. Knoop got one of each and milk.

"I thought you weren't hungry," Burke said.

"I missed breakfast," Knoop said.

"Leave room for dessert. I saw some nice vanilla cake with a sweet frosting," Burke said.

A bit later, as Knoop and Burke ate slices of vanilla cake, a telegraph operator entered the cafeteria and rushed to the table.

The operator handed Burke a telegram.

Burke scanned it quickly and then looked at Knoop.

"Let's go," Burke said.

"Our search of the Register of Deeds has given us Robert Wood, a jury member on the Stuyvesant trial," Burke said. "He left New York with his wife about five years ago and purchased a small ranch in Wyoming."

"Wyoming?" Arthur said. "He left the biggest city in the country for a Godforsaken wasteland?"

159

"Wood is originally from New Mexico Territory, so perhaps he wanted to return to his roots after he retired?" Burke suggested.

"The others?" Arthur said.

"Not yet," Burke said.

"Wait until the end of the business day. There might be others forthcoming," Arthur said. "In the morning, I will send a team of Secret Service agents to Wyoming to place the Wood family in protective custody."

"Mr. Burke, this is from the Register of Deeds in Colorado," a telegraph operator said.

Burke took the telegram and he and Knoop read it together.

"Melvin, you may take this one yourself," Burke said.

"To the president?" Knoop said.

"Yes, the president. I doubt housekeeping would be much interested," Burke said.

Knoop took the telegram to the Oval Office where Arthur was drinking coffee and studying blueprints at his desk.

"Railroad expansion plans," Arthur said. "Is there anything more tedious than looking at railroad expansion plans?"

"Yes, sir. Sir, we located another member of the jury," Knoop said and handed Arthur the telegram.

"J. Douglas Turner, Colorado," Arthur said. "The Town of Glenwood?"

"Yes, sir, that's what it says," Knoop said.

"Melvin, you and Burke report to me after the close of the business day," Arthur said.

As Murphy and his father stepped down off the train, both stretched their backs and cracked their necks in unison. Each had a pipe clenched between his lips.

Behind them, Aideen and Kai exchanged grins.

Michael's foreman was waiting for them at the end of the platform with a carriage.

"Our place is closer," Michael said to Murphy and Kai. "You can stay with us the night, and I'll ride you over in the morning."

"If the general store is still open in town, stop for bread," Aideen said. "We won't have time to bake a fresh loaf."

By the time Burke and Knoop met Arthur for the meeting in the Oval Office, a third member of the missing five jury members had surfaced.

"Donald Craig left Manhattan six years ago and purchased a small ranch in Utah," Burke said. "In Mormon country."

"Two jury members left, sir," Knoop said. "If they purchased a home or property, we'll know by late afternoon tomorrow."

"Excellent work, Melvin," Arthur said.

"I can't take credit for Mr. Murphy's plan, sir," Knoop said.

"Of course not. I will," Arthur said.

Knoop looked at Arthur with raised eyebrows.

"Don't look so shocked, Melvin," Arthur said. "It's how the game of politics is played. Old men start wars and young men fight and die in them, and the old men take credit for victory and the shame of defeat. History doesn't remember the foot soldiers, just the kings and presidents. Remember that, Melvin."

"Yes, sir."

"Tomorrow, William, send a team of agents to Glenwood in Colorado and put the Turner family into protective custody," Arthur said. "Send telegrams to US marshals to do the same for the Craig and the Wood families, but Turner is a priority."

"May I ask why Turner is a priority over the others?" Burke said.

"Glenwood Springs. Ever hear of it?" Arthur said.

"I can't say as I have," Burke said.

161

"People believe the hot springs have some kind of medicinal benefits," Arthur said. "I read once that after the O.K. Corral shooting, Doc Holliday went to Glenwood for his tuberculosis. Turner or his wife may be ill and using the hot springs for treatment."

"Sir, I would like to go with the team to Glenwood," Knoop said.

"Melvin, you are not a field agent," Arthur said.

"I rode all across the west with Murphy a year ago when we tracked the Japanese criminals bringing in counterfeit money," Knoop said.

"He did, sir," Burke said. "I think Melvin has earned the right to go to Glenwood."

Arthur sighed. "All right, Melvin, but you stay in the background and let the field agents carry the load."

Knoop grinned. "I will, sir."

"As a precaution, I think we should wire the local sheriff in Glenwood and ask him to provide security until our people arrive," Burke said. "After all, it will take three days to get there."

"I'll send the telegram myself," Arthur said.

"What's on your mind, son?" Michael said.

Murphy took a sip of bourbon and shook his head. "Nothing, Dad. I'm fine."

They were on the porch of Michael's house after dark. Each had a glass of whiskey and his pipe.

"A long time ago when you joined the army and went off to war, the day you told your mother and me, you had this look on your face," Michael said. "Guilt was the look you wore that day. You're wearing that same look now."

Murphy took a sip of bourbon and sighed. "Kai is my wife. She needs me, and I need her. We want to build a life together, and we're off to a pretty good start. A man rarely gets more than one chance to correct his mistakes."

"But?"

"I feel a bit . . . guilty about leaving in the middle of an investigation," Murphy said.

"You're not the only Secret Service agent, you know," Michael said. "And you've more than done your duty for this country. Besides, from what I understand of it, you did exactly what you signed on to do, so you didn't leave in the middle of anything."

"I know," Murphy said. "I expect I'll feel much better when I start the campaign for Congress in a few weeks."

"You got my vote, son," Michael said.

"You're not in the Fort Smith district," Murphy said.

"I won't tell if you don't," Michael said. "Let's go in and see what our women are up to."

Knoop was in his room at the White House, packing for the trip west when Burke knocked on the door.

"Come in," Knoop said.

Burke opened the door and entered the room, carrying a briefcase.

"There is a nice apartment available in a brownstone building less than a mile from the White House," Burke said. "I reserved it for you to look at when you return."

"Thank you, Mr. Burke," Knoop said.

"Melvin, do you own a gun?" Burke said.

"A gun? Just the standard issue Mr. Pinkerton gave me. A Smith and Wesson .38," Knoop said. "I left it in Chicago."

Burke set the briefcase on the bed and opened it. He removed a Colt revolver and shoulder holster.

"Standard issue for Secret Service agents," Burke said.

"I'll be with a team, Mr. Burke. I doubt I'll need it," Knoop said.

"It's mandatory an agent in the field be armed," Burke said. "Keep it holstered if you like, but wear it."

Knoop took the heavy Colt revolver and nodded.

"Thank you, Mr. Burke," he said.

"You're welcome, Melvin," Burke said. "Get some rest; you have a long train ride ahead."

"Yes, sir," Knoop said.

After Burke left the room, Knoop removed the heavy Colt revolver from the shoulder holster and held it in his rather small hand.

"If I have to use this, the only one I'm going to hurt is me," he said and returned the Colt to the holster.

CHAPTER TWENTY-TWO

Murphy and Kai rode to the north fields on Murphy's Tennessee farm. Murphy rode his beloved, massive horse, Boyle, while Kai rode her much smaller pinto for which she had yet to provide a name.

They dismounted and walked a bit through the tall cornstalks.

"My father will be very pleased about this crop," Murphy said. "He was hoping for four hundred barrels this year, but it's likely to be five."

"And are you pleased?" Kai said.

"Yes. I was also thinking that now that our home in Fort Smith is complete, we could take that honeymoon before I start campaigning for Congress," Murphy said.

"Where shall we go?" Kai asked.

"I'll leave that to you," Murphy said. "Pick a place you've never been but always wanted to see, and that is where we will go."

"Can I study on that for a bit?" Kai said.

"Sure, but don't take too long," Murphy said. "I might actually win a seat in Congress."

The ride to Colorado would take three days and nights. On the fourth day, the scheduled arrival time was eight in the morning.

A station was scheduled to be completed in Glenwood in a few years, but the closest the train could take them this time was a full day's ride from the hot springs.

Knoop studied a map in his sleeper car.

On the map, Glenwood Springs was called Defiance. It was established as a town just about a year ago, even though people had been visiting the hot springs for decades. Hundreds of years, if you counted Native Americans.

Knoop could find no reason why Turner moved to Glenwood. It had to be, as President Arthur suspected, for health reasons.

Either his or his wife's.

Was Stuyvesant smart enough to know that?

It seemed to Knoop that Stuyvesant was a very smart man, smart enough to fool the police and commit eight murders right under their noses.

If it wasn't for Murphy, they'd still be at a loss as to how Stuyvesant located the jury members and judge.

There was a soft knock on Knoop's sleeping car door.

"Melvin, it's Wise. We're going to the dining car for some dinner. Join us," Agent Wise said.

"Save me a seat. I'll be there in a minute," Knoop said.

Knoop closed the map and his notebook. He washed his face in the basin on the table, combed his hair, put his suit jacket on, and then left the car.

Agent in Charge Wise wasn't much older than Knoop at thirty-five. He was tall, although not as tall as Murphy, and while he was considered a top agent, Knoop knew Wise was no substitute for Murphy's experience or physical prowess.

Knoop joined Wise and four other agents at a table in the dining car.

"Two more days to Denver," Wise said. "Then a short ride north to Defiance to pick up the Turner family and take them into custody at Fort Collins. Easy work, Melvin."

Knoop nodded. Wise was something else that Murphy was not: cocky.

"The waiter recommended the baked chicken. I ordered it for us all," Wise said. "I hope you don't mind."

"Not at all," Knoop said.

"Good God, William, it's after midnight," Arthur said when he opened the residence door. "Don't you ever sleep?"

"Not tonight, Mr. President," Burke said.

"Well, what is it?" Arthur said.

"From Pittsburgh," Burke said. He handed Arthur a telegram from the chief of police.

Arthur scanned the telegram quickly.

"My worst fear has come to pass," Arthur said. "A copycat killer in Pittsburgh."

"It appears so, Mr. President," Burke said.

"Is it too late to ask for a blackout in the newspapers?" Arthur said.

"It will be in all the major papers first thing tomorrow," Burke said.

Arthur sighed heavily. "Come in, William. Let's have a drink," Arthur said. "I know I could use one."

Murphy sat alone on the porch of his Tennessee house, smoked his pipe, and sipped bourbon from a small glass.

The wall-mounted oil lantern was on low flame.

As he sipped whiskey, Kai, wearing a robe, stepped out and said, "I woke up. You were gone. Is something wrong?"

"No," Murphy said. "I'm just . . . reflecting."

"Reflecting?" Kai said.

"It's nothing. Don't worry about it," Murphy said.

Kai sat on Murphy's lap and said, "Tell me."

"A man doesn't often get a second chance like I've been given," Murphy said. "I've been thinking what I did to deserve such good luck in having a woman like you come along and

167

want to be my wife."

"Oh, I admit you can be rough around the edges sometimes, but you're not so hard to take in general," Kai said. "Besides, we've both had a rough time of it, so maybe we're due for some smooth sailing, as they say."

"Have you given any thought to where you want to spend our honeymoon?" Murphy said.

"How long will it take to travel to Seattle?"

"From Tennessee? About four days and nights by train."

"I was reading about Alaska," Kai said. "They have ships that take tourists to Alaska to see the icebergs and wildlife and the Northern Lights."

"I've always wanted to see the Northern Lights," Murphy said.

"Let's go to bed and talk about it," Kai said.

"Talk?"

Kai stood up and took Murphy's hand. "Or something," she said.

"What a mess," Arthur said.

Burke took a sip of bourbon. "It is that, sir," he said.

"We'll never get anyone to sit on a jury once this story hits the public, and I don't blame them," Arthur said.

"I dread the stock market reports at the close of business tomorrow," Burke said.

"On top of everything else, there is that," Arthur said. "It's amazing the damage one man can cause when he sets his mind to it."

"Washington was one man," Burke said. "So was Napoleon, Alexander the Great, and Emperor Charlemagne."

"And John Wilkes Booth," Arthur said.

"Are you suggesting Stuyvesant is your John Wilkes Booth?" Burke said.

Arthur sipped from his glass and then looked across the kitchen table at Burke. "Is there anybody in the Secret Service capable of finding Stuyvesant?"

"Doubtful, sir," Burke said.

"What about the US marshals?"

"From which state or territory?" Burke said. "At best, we can issue wanted posters with Stuyvesant's picture on them."

"Could Murphy find this—?"

"Yes."

"Could we—?"

"Probably not," Burke said. "But if this isn't resolved by next week when I see him in Fort Smith, I'll mention it."

"I'll get him into the Senate," Arthur said.

Burke grinned.

"What?" Arthur said.

"I doubt Murphy can be bribed, Mr. President," Burke said.

"Why is it the best killers of men always have a conscience?" Arthur said.

When Knoop awoke, the train was at a stopover in Topeka, Kansas. He washed quickly at the basin, put on a clean shirt, and left his room in a hurry. He found Agent Wise and the men having coffee in the dining car.

"There you are, Melvin," Wise said. "All we can get until the train leaves the station is coffee. Join us."

Knoop sat and a waiter brought him a cup of coffee.

"One more night on this dreaded train, Melvin," Wise said.

"Where can we get horses in Denver?" Knoop said.

"Mr. Burke reserved six horses at a Denver livery," Wise said.

"What about the Turner family?" Knoop said.

"I'm sure they have a wagon or horses," Wise said.

"How long of a layover do we have?" Knoop said.

"The conductor said an hour," Wise said.

"I'm going out and getting a newspaper," Knoop said.

"Mom, Dad, come to Fort Smith and help with my campaign next month," Murphy said.

"I don't know what good we could do," Michael said.

Aideen looked at Kai, and Kai nodded softly.

"I'm sure Mr. Burke can find some things we can do to help," Aideen said. "We'll be there when you send for us."

Murphy shook hands with Michael and kissed Aideen on the cheek. Kai hugged and kissed Aideen and Michael.

"Have a safe trip," Michael said.

Murphy helped Kai into the saddle of her pinto, then mounted Boyle.

As they rode away, Murphy said, "Have you picked a name for your horse yet?"

Knoop found Wise and his team having coffee in the dining car when he returned to the train after picking up a copy of the Kansas City and Topeka newspapers.

Knoop set the papers on the table in front of Wise.

"Copycat killer is what they are calling a man who shot and killed a jury member in Pittsburgh," Knoop said.

Wise looked at the newspapers.

"Our mission is to place the Turner family into federal protective custody," Wise said. "We can't afford to get sidetracked on another issue."

"I think we should wire Mr. Burke from Denver," Knoop said.

Wise glanced at the newspapers and nodded.

"All right, Melvin," Wise said. "But for now, let's order breakfast."

Chapter Twenty-Three

Murphy and Kai led their horses from the railroad station to the center of Fort Smith. It was an hour before sunset, and the streets were caught in an eerie glow.

Murphy said, "Let's pick up supplies before the general store closes and spend the night in our new home."

"The only clothes I have are in my carry satchel," Kai said. "You, too."

"It's enough for tonight," Murphy said. "We'll ride back in the morning and rent a wagon and pick up everything we left behind at the boarding house."

They walked the horses to the general store where they purchased forty pounds of supplies. Murphy draped the two sacks over Boyle's saddle and they rode to their house ten miles outside of town.

At the house, Murphy carried the supplies into the house after Kai used her key to unlock the heavy door.

"I'll tend to the horses," Murphy said.

Stacked neatly on the side of the house were the wood, posts, and posthole diggers to build the corral, a project Murphy intended to start tomorrow. For tonight, Boyle and Kai's horse would spend the night tied to the hitching post in front of the porch.

Murphy removed the saddles and blankets and took them to the porch, along with his Winchester rifle. As he brushed and groomed the horses, he caught the aroma of chicken being fried in a pan.

As Murphy walked up to the porch, the screen door opened and Kai came out with two mugs of coffee. She gave him a cup, and they took chairs.

"When we get back from town, I'll get started on the corral," Murphy said. "It shouldn't take too long, but we'll need to contact the company we hired to build the house to build the barn."

"I have to see Judge Parker tomorrow," Kai said. "The school year starts in the fall. If I'm to teach the children on the reservation, I need to be ready."

"What about Alaska?" Murphy said.

"Plenty of time for that if we don't wait too long," Kai said.

"You're forgetting I'm to start campaigning in a month," Murphy said.

"Then I suggest we leave for Alaska inside of a week," Kai said.

Murphy nodded. "We'll stop by the railroad on the way to town," Murphy said.

"Supper is keeping warm," Kai said.

"Then let's eat," Murphy said. "Before it gets cold."

Wise called a meeting after the dining car closed for the evening, although coffee was still available. As he, the four agents, and Knoop gathered at a table, each man filled a cup with coffee before taking a seat.

Wise unfolded a map and spread it out on the table.

"When we reach Denver in the morning, we will pick up our horses at the livery stable and then board a construction train that will take us to within an hour's ride south of Defiance, or Glenwood Springs, as it is commonly known. After we pick up the Turner family, it's a two-day ride to Fort Collins. Once the

Turner family is safely in custody, I'll wire Mr. Burke for additional orders. If there are none, we'll head back to Washington."

"What about Pittsburgh?" Knoop said.

Wise looked at Knoop. "What about it?"

"As Pittsburgh is on our way back to Washington, perhaps Mr. Burke would like us to check out the copycat shooting?" Knoop said.

"Yes, he might at that," Wise said. "I'll mention it to Mr. Burke when I send the wire."

Arthur wasn't at his desk fifteen minutes when Burke knocked on the door and entered carrying several telegrams.

"We've located the remaining two families," Burke said. "Clinton, according to the Register of Deeds, purchased a small ranch north of Dallas. Olson purchased a small ranch in Nevada, where he is from originally."

"When do you expect the team to reach Glenwood?" Arthur said.

"By early this afternoon."

"Wire the fort commander at Collins and have Wise telegraph immediately when the team arrives," Arthur said. "I want them to respond to each of the remaining four families and have them all placed in protective custody."

"I already did," Burke said.

"Of course you did," Arthur said. "Have you had breakfast yet?"

Knoop picked up a copy of the Denver newspaper while he and his fellow agents waited for the special train to arrive.

The front page story wasn't good. It detailed events about the Pittsburgh shooting of a jury member.

The jury wasn't sequestered during the trial of a man arrested for murder. The trial was in its second week. After the close of court for the day, a man followed a jury member home and shot him in the back of the head.

A note was left on the body.

Not Guilty Or More Will Die.

Knoop showed the newspaper to Wise.

"I'm sure Mr. Burke will want us to stop in Pittsburgh after this," Wise said.

Behind Knoop, the special train arrived. It consisted of an engine car, riding car, and boxcar for the horses.

"Let's get the horses loaded," Wise said.

"Hello, Kai, Murphy. What brings you to my courthouse?" Judge Parker said.

"I wanted to talk to you about starting teaching on the reservation this fall," Kai said.

"I'm glad you stopped by," Parker said. "This came for you about a week ago."

He slid open a desk drawer and produced an envelope.

"It's your teaching license from the Department of Indian Affairs," Parker said.

Kai opened the envelope and smiled at Parker. "I will do my best to educate the children," she said.

"I know you will," Parker said. "The school year starts right after the fall harvest and runs until late spring. Three days a week, five hours a day. I'd like to arrange a meeting with the Indian Agent for the reservation so you can get to know each other."

Kai looked at Murphy. "We can ride out to the reservation and meet the Indian Agent whenever you say, Judge," she said.

"I'll get word to you tomorrow," Parker said. "Are you staying in town? I thought we could have lunch."

"We've got a wagon full of clothes downstairs, but nothing

that won't keep," Murphy said.

"Let me get my jacket," Parker said.

After Knoop, Wise, and the team walked their horses from the boxcar, the conductor said, "Follow the road for about ten miles straight to Defiance."

"We will. Thanks," Wise said.

They waited for the train to back up, then mounted the horses and followed the road to Defiance.

The Colorado scenery was beautiful. Knoop took it all in as they rode at a moderate pace.

As they neared the springs in the mountains, they reached a sign that read *Glenwood Springs one mile.*

When they finally arrived at the springs, Knoop was a bit surprised at how big a complex it was. A large hotel and several smaller bungalows surrounded the acres of hot springs that had been walled in to create a pool. Telegraph poles connected the hotel to the telegraph lines.

A dozen or more bathers were in the springs when they dismounted at the hotel.

"I'll check the hotel to see if the Turners are registered," Wise said. "If not, we'll ride out to their residence, which, according to Mr. Burke, isn't very far from here."

While Wise was in the hotel, Knoop wandered closer to the springs. He could smell the sulfur is the air from the hot, mineral water people were bathing in.

On the opposite side of the pool there were several bungalows with the mountains as a backdrop.

Curious about the pool, Knoop walked around it to the other side where the bungalows stood.

He looked at the mountains in the background.

The air was filled with the aroma of sulfur as a breeze came down from the mountains and stirred the fumes rising from the pool.

Soft voices from the pool sounded quietly in the background.

What a wonderful place, Knoop thought just as a gunshot sounded and echoed loudly throughout the mountains.

The shot came from a bungalow.

Knoop froze for a second or two, and then raced up a slight hill toward the bungalows. As he neared the bungalows, he reached into his jacket and pulled the Colt revolver from the shoulder holster.

Knoop paused in shock when John Stuyvesant backed out of a bungalow with the .36 caliber Navy Colt in his right hand. He turned and walked toward a horse tethered to a nearby tree.

Knoop ran to Stuyvesant.

"Stop," Knoop shouted. "You're under arrest."

Stuyvesant turned and looked at Knoop. Stuyvesant's hair was shoulder length, he wore a thick, dark beard, and he was dressed as a cowboy.

There was just a brief second of eye contact, but Knoop saw the rage and insanity in Stuyvesant's eyes.

Stuyvesant looked at the Colt in Knoop's right hand.

Without hesitation, Stuyvesant cocked the Navy Colt and shot Knoop in the left side of his chest.

Knoop was blown off his feet by the powerful ball and landed on his back. He knew he had been shot. He could see the hole and the flowing blood, yet it was nothing like he expected.

For one thing, there was very little pain. He attributed that to shock.

The other thing was how clear and crisp everything seemed. He watched as Stuyvesant mounted his horse and rode quickly toward the mountains. He looked up at nearby trees and saw the tops blowing softly in the mountain breeze. It was as if he could see every leaf on every branch as they gently rocked back and forth. Above the trees, the sky was bluer than he had ever seen it, and the clouds seemed like giant puffs of whipped cream.

"Melvin! Ah, Jesus," Wise said.

"I'm okay. I just need to catch my breath. I'll be all right in a minute," Knoop said. "It was Stuyvesant. I saw him come out of a bungalow."

"There's a doctor at the hotel," Wise said. "One of you run back and get him. The rest of you help me stop the bleeding."

"I'll be all right in a minute," Knoop said. "I just need to catch my breath."

"I know, Melvin. I know," Wise said.

"Who would want to kill Mr. Turner?" the doctor said to Wise as he stopped the bleeding in Knoop's chest.

"You don't get the newspapers out here much, do you, doctor?" Wise said.

"We don't want our visitors to experience needless stress," the doctor said. "They are here for their health, after all."

"Well, right now Turner is dead and Melvin is alive," Wise said. "I'd like to keep him that way."

"The bullet will need to come out," the doctor said.

"Then take it out," Wise said.

"It's not that easy," the doctor said. "It's lodged in his lung. He'll require a really fine surgeon to get it out."

"Will he survive a wagon ride to Denver?" Wise said.

"If I went with you," the doctor said.

"Pack your bag," Wise said.

"Mrs. Turner is heavily sedated," the doctor said. "She'll need me."

"Mrs. Turner is alive. Melvin might not be," Wise said. "Pack your bag. Then have a telegram sent to the Denver railroad to meet us at the spot where they dropped us off."

177

CHAPTER TWENTY-FOUR

After breakfast, Murphy began digging postholes to build the corral. Each post stood seven feet tall, and each hole had to go down one foot. Once the hole was dug, Murphy placed the pointed end of the post into it and used a heavy wood mallet to pound it a foot deeper into the ground.

Murphy worked quickly, and within an hour had six posts set in place. He was using the posthole digger to make the seventh hole when Judge Parker arrived in his buggy.

"It's a fine, beautiful house, Murphy," Parker said as he stepped down from his buggy.

"It is that," Murphy said.

Kai stepped onto the porch, carrying a picnic basket. She wore a long blue skirt, black shoes with a one-inch heel, and a white, pinstriped blouse. A tiny handbag was slung over her right shoulder.

"I made us a picnic lunch for the trip," Kai said as she approached Parker.

"That's very thoughtful of you, Kai," Parker said.

Kai turned to Murphy. "Try not to kill yourself today building the corral," she said.

"Don't worry. I'll have it finished by suppertime," Murphy said.

Parker helped Kai into the buggy and as they rode away, Parker said, "Is he serious?"

"That he'll have it finished by suppertime?" Kai said. "Very much so."

Kai looked back to see Murphy pounding a post with the wood mallet. She faced forward and grinned.

The doctor covered the cab of the wagon with a thick layer of hay, and then spread out six wool blankets to cushion the ride. Wise and several others lifted Knoop into the wagon and gently set him down.

"Is he asleep?" Wise said.

"Sedated," the doctor said. "I'll need you to ride in the back with me so we can keep him steady."

Once underway, the doctor checked Knoop's pulse and temperature every half hour.

"He has a fever, which is to be expected with the bullet still in him, but I don't want him to have a seizure," the doctor said. "There's a canteen and some towels there in the corner. Grab them for me."

Wise grabbed the canteen and towels and gave them to the doctor. The doctor wet a towel and wiped Knoop's face with it.

"How far to the place the railroad will pick us up?" the doctor said.

Wise looked into the distance and spotted tiny puffs of black smoke. "About an hour," he said.

Murphy was sitting in a chair on the porch with a mug of coffee and his pipe when a buggy arrived with US Marshal Cal Witson driving and Kai seated next to him.

As Witson helped Kai step down from the buggy, she looked at Boyle and her horse inside the newly completed corral.

Murphy stood and greeted Kai with a kiss on the cheek and Witson with a handshake.

"Something smells pretty damn good," Witson said.

"That's beef stew," Murphy said. "And a bed of Chinese rice. And yes, there is more than enough for three."

"Well, the judge has night court tonight, but a man has got to eat," Witson said.

"Come in," Kai said. "I'll show you where you can wash."

Wise and the doctor sat in the Denver hospital waiting room while a resident surgeon examined Knoop.

After about an hour, the surgeon came into the waiting room. Wise and the doctor stood up.

"The only surgeon I know of who can remove the bullet from Mr. Knoop is Doctor Henry Bloom, and he is in Washington, giving a lecture at Georgetown University at the moment."

"Can he be transported to Washington?" Wise said. "By train?"

"In a sleeper car perhaps, but a doctor and nurse will have to make the trip with him," the surgeon said.

"I'm a doctor. Can you spare a hospital nurse?" the doctor said.

"I suppose so," the surgeon said.

"Where can I send a telegram?" Wise said.

Burke handed the lengthy telegram to Arthur, who sat behind his desk in the Oval Office.

Arthur read the telegram quickly and then looked at Burke.

"Recommendations?" Arthur said.

"The railroad is federal and at your command," Burke said. "Have Denver prepare a three-car train and order it to transport Knoop to Washington. Top speed all the way, and it's to make no stops except for water and coal. I'll go to Georgetown and have this Doctor Bloom stay in Washington to perform the surgery."

"Send one telegram to the railroad in Denver and one to that hospital, and then get over to Georgetown University," Arthur said.

Burke nodded and quickly left the Oval Office.

Once Knoop was safely in the bed inside a sleeper car, the train slowly rolled forward and away from the Denver railroad platform.

The doctor and a nurse from the hospital stayed with Knoop, while Wise and his team went to the riding car. A team of three engineers were assigned by the railroad. Two were in the riding car.

"With no stops except for water and coal, we can be in Washington in sixty hours," an engineer said. "But you lads will have to shovel coal and ride with the engineer."

"We'll take turns," Wise said.

The riding car was equipped with a small kitchen area. Wise fired up the small stove and made a pot of coffee. When it was ready, he filled two large mugs and took them to the sleeping car.

"How is he?" Wise asked.

"No change, which is actually good news," the doctor said. "He seems to have stabilized. We need to keep him that way for the rest of the trip."

Wise looked at his pocket watch. "That's another fifty-nine hours at least," he said.

The doctor looked at Knoop. "He doesn't want to die," he said. "So we should do whatever it takes to make sure he doesn't."

"The train is in route and should arrive in about fifty-four hours," Burke said.

Arthur nodded. "And Doctor Bloom?"

"He's agreed to stay in Washington and perform the operation at Saint Elizabeth's Hospital," Burke said.

"All we can do now is wait," Arthur said.

"I should wire Murphy with the news."

"No," Arthur said.

"Murphy will want to know," Burke said.

"Wait until the train arrives in Washington and then wire Murphy," Arthur said.

Burke looked at Arthur. "Murphy will be furious, Mr. President," he said.

"Exactly what I'm counting on, William," Arthur said.

"How is he?" Wise said.

"His fever has spiked," the doctor said. "I requested a block of ice be brought on board. It's wrapped in burlap in the kitchen area. Break it up with an ice pick, fill a basin, and hurry."

Wise went to the riding car and found the block of ice under the counter. He unwrapped it, chipped off enough ice with a pick to fill a basin, and brought the basin to the sleeping car.

"We'll take it from here," the doctor said.

"Can you make a pot of coffee for the doctor and me?" the nurse said.

Wise nodded and returned to the riding car. It was the middle of the night, and three of his men and two engineers were asleep in their seats. He made a pot of coffee and took it to the sleeper car, returned to the riding car, and made another pot.

When the second pot was ready, he took it and three cups to the engineer driving the train. One of his men was shoveling coal into the furnace.

Wise filled three cups and gave one to the engineer and his agent.

"Forty hours to Washington," the engineer said.

CHAPTER TWENTY-FIVE

Kai prepared a lunch of fried chicken with potatoes, bread, and lemonade. When the portable table was set up with tablecloth and a dozen plates, she rang the dinner bell.

The contractor from Little Rock, Mr. Grillo, and a dozen of his crew, plus Murphy, nearly had the barn completed.

At the sound of the bell, the men broke from their work and came to the outdoor pump to wash before coming to the table.

"I made enough to feed a small army, and I don't expect one leftover scrap," Kai said.

"Your husband is a small army all by himself," Grillo said.

"Eat," Kai said. "I have a pie for dessert that is ready to come out of the oven."

Work stopped at five in the afternoon. Grillo and his crew had a hotel in Fort Smith where they had been staying the past two nights. His men were anxious for baths and a visit to a saloon.

"This time tomorrow, she'll be complete," Grillo said.

After Grillo and his crew left, Kai prepared a hot bath for Murphy.

He was soaking in the bath when Marshal Cal Witson knocked on the front door.

"Marshal Witson, is something wrong?" Kai said when she answered the door.

"The telegraph office took this telegram to Judge Parker, and he ordered me to deliver it in person," Witson said.

Kai took the telegram and read it quickly. "Thank you, Marshal, I'll take it to Murphy right away."

"Good night, Kai," Witson said.

Kai took the telegram to the bedroom. There she removed the train schedule from a dresser drawer and then took the telegram to Murphy, who was still in the tub.

"From Burke," Kai said.

Murphy took the telegram and read it quickly.

Melvin Knoop was shot by Stuyvesant in Glenwood Springs. Arrived today in Washington for emergency surgery at Saint Elizabeth's Hospital. His condition is critical. William Burke.

Murphy stood up, stepped out of the tub, and took the large towel Kai handed him.

"I'll need to get a train schedule," he said.

"A train leaves at midnight and arrives in Washington at nine in the morning," Kai said. "For how long should I pack?"

Doctor Bloom, two assisting surgeons, and three nurses operated on Knoop at noon. They worked tirelessly for five hours.

The .36 caliber ball had broken a rib in two, entered the left lung, and was resting against the rear of the lung against the backside of the rib cage.

It took all of Bloom's skill and endurance to perform the operation. Exhausted, he left his assistants and nurses to sew up the long cut in Knoop's chest.

Bloom found Wise and Burke in the waiting room.

"The operation went well," Bloom said. "But Knoop's condition is still critical for now. He's a fighter, for sure, but he lost a great deal of blood."

"But he will make it?" Burke said.

"If he is alive come morning, he will make it," Bloom said.

Kai waited for Murphy to finish dressing. He wore a dark suit with a frock coat and his regular Stetson hat.

When he strapped on his black Colt Peacemaker, she knew the ride to Washington would be long and quiet.

"We'll board the horses in town," was all he said until they were on the train and heading for Washington.

Then he said, "When I purchased the tickets, I paid for a sleeper car so you can get some rest."

"I'll sit here with you," Kai said.

"All night?"

"If you sit, I sit," Kai said.

Murphy sighed. "All right. Let's try to get some sleep then."

"Knoop pulled through the surgery, but we won't know for sure if he'll make it until morning," Burke said.

"And Murphy?" Arthur said.

"He wired me from the Fort Smith railroad station," Burke said. "He'll be here around nine tomorrow morning."

"Go home, get some rest, and pick Murphy up at the station," Arthur said.

"He'll be more than furious, Mr. President."

Arthur nodded. "Like I said, I'm counting on it," he said.

Carrying two suitcases, Murphy walked beside Kai along the platform at the Washington railroad station.

"There is Mr. Burke," Kai said.

When they reached the end of the platform, Burke said, "The president is waiting for—"

"The hell with the president," Murphy said. "If you want to put your carriage to good use, take us to the hospital and tell us what happened along the way."

Burke looked at Kai.

"Might as well, or he'll just walk to the hospital," Kai said.

"Get in," Burke said.

Burke led Murphy and Kai into the waiting room of Saint Elizabeth's Hospital, where Wise was waiting in a chair.

Wise stood and said, "Mr. Burke, I was hoping you would show up."

Murphy walked past Burke and looked at Wise. "Are you Agent Wise?"

"Yes, who are—?" Wise said.

Murphy grabbed Wise by the throat and shoved him against the wall. Others in the waiting room immediately rushed out.

"You stupid son of a bitch! You don't let a man walk into a trap when in the field," Murphy said. "Especially an inexperienced man."

Wise grabbed Murphy's arm, but Murphy's grip was a vise, and Wise was powerless to break free.

"Murphy, for God's sake, let him go," Burke said.

Murphy shook Wise as if he were a child's doll and said, "If Melvin dies, so do you."

Burke turned to Kai.

"Better rein him in," Burke said.

Kai stepped between Murphy and Wise. "I thought we came here to see Melvin," she said.

Murphy released Wise. Wise slumped to the floor with his back against the wall.

Kai took Murphy's hand. "Let's go see Melvin," she said.

As Kai and Murphy left the waiting room, Burke helped Wise to his feet.

"Who was that?" Wise said.

"Murphy, and I'd stay clear of him if I were you," Burke said.

"No shit," Wise gasped.

★ ★ ★ ★ ★

Knoop lay in a private room on the second floor. He was unconscious when Murphy, Kai, and Burke entered.

Kai took the chair beside the bed and held Knoop's hand.

"He was always so happy to see me," she said and started to cry.

Doctor Bloom entered the room and said, "I thought I saw you, Mr. Burke."

"How is he?" Burke said.

"Alive," Bloom said. "He has a fever and an infection, but that usually follows a gunshot wound and surgery."

"You did the surgery?" Murphy said.

"I did," Bloom said.

"Thank you," Murphy said. "According to Burke, you're one of the few men in the country who could have."

"I'm just glad I could do it," Bloom said. "But right now he needs rest and quiet."

"We need to see the president anyway," Burke said.

"Doctor, let me sit with him for a while," Kai said. "I won't disturb him."

Bloom nodded. "All right, but just for a little while."

"Through the Register of Deeds, as you suggested, we located the remaining jury members," Arthur said. "We have them in protective custody. The bigger problem is the copycat killers, one in Pittsburgh, and another as of last night in Boston."

"By now Stuyvesant is aware he's being hunted and will go into hiding, if he hasn't already done so," Murphy said.

"The bigger picture is that the country is very close to a recession the likes of seventy-three over this," Arthur said. "Millions of people will be hurt economically if things don't turn around and soon."

Burke looked at Murphy. "What are you prepared to do?" he said.

"Is that agent outside?" Murphy said.

"Wise?" Burke said. "In the hall."

"Get him," Murphy said.

Burke went to the door, opened it, and waved to Wise. Wise entered the Oval Office, and Burke closed the door.

"Do you know the exact location where Knoop was shot?" Murphy said.

Wise nodded. "I do."

"We'll leave in three days," Murphy said. "I'll pick you up here."

Wise looked at Arthur.

"You heard the man," Arthur said.

"I'd like to borrow your train for the ride west," Murphy said to Arthur. "Express with a clear track. We've lost enough time as it is."

"I'll make sure it's ready," Arthur said.

"So you're going after the man then?" Kai said.

"Yes," Murphy said.

"It changes all our plans," Kai said.

"Just temporarily. Are you angry?"

"Yes, but not at you," Kai said. "At the man who shot Melvin. I expect you to bring him to justice for Melvin's sake."

"Our honeymoon?"

"Will just have to wait until you return," Kai said.

"I've gone back on my word," Murphy said.

"If you hadn't, I would have asked you to," Kai said.

"I feel better knowing you approve," Murphy said.

"I approve, and the Navajo in me wants justice," Kai said. "The Irish in me wants vengeance. Understand?"

"Yes."

Murphy looked at Knoop, who was still unconscious in his bed.

"I think he'll make it," he said.

"The doctor said he has a good chance," Kai said.

"I wired my parents to meet us in Fort Smith," Murphy said. "Our train leaves in two hours. We have time for some lunch if you'd like."

Kai nodded. "Let me say goodbye to Melvin first."

Burke filled two glasses with whiskey and handed one to Arthur, who sat behind his desk.

"In case you are wondering, William, I don't feel the least bit bad for manipulating Murphy the way I did."

"I wasn't, and Murphy can't be made to do something he doesn't want to do in the first place," Burke said. "Not by me or you, or even his wife."

Arthur sipped. Burke sipped. Quiet reigned for a few seconds.

"Do you think Murphy will find Stuyvesant?" Arthur said.

"Oh yes," Burke said. "And heaven help that man when Murphy knocks on his door."

Arthur nodded. "In the morning, make sure my train is ready to go and is well stocked," he said.

CHAPTER TWENTY-SIX

Michael was on the porch of the new house in Fort Smith, sipping whiskey and smoking his pipe when he spotted Murphy and Kai on horseback.

The moon was close to full, and there was no mistaking Murphy's outline atop his massive horse, Boyle.

Michael stood when they reached the hitching post.

"Hello, Dad," Murphy said. "Thanks for coming."

Murphy dismounted and then helped Kai from the saddle.

"Is Ma asleep?" Murphy said.

"She's in the kitchen keeping supper warm," Michael said. "We didn't get here but two hours ago."

"I'll go help her," Kai said.

After Kai entered the house, Murphy sat next to his father.

"I got an extra glass here," Michael said and filled it with whiskey.

Murphy took the glass and sipped. "Thanks, Dad."

"So where are you off to?" Michael said.

"Colorado, and then I don't know," Murphy said. "The man shot Knoop and left him for dead. I owe it to Knoop to find Stuyvesant and bring him in to answer for what he's done."

"And your wife?" Michael said.

"She agrees I need to do this," Murphy said.

Michael puffed on his pipe for a few seconds. "What's on your mind, son?"

"I'd like you to stay with Kai until I return," Murphy said.

"She is a strong, capable woman, but company helps pass the time."

"I understand," Michael said. "When will you leave?"

"In the morning."

Kai opened the screen door and poked her head out. "Aideen went to a lot of trouble to fix supper. The least you men can do is come in and eat it."

Kai sat in front of her dresser and brushed her long, dark hair. She looked in the mirror at Murphy, who was prone on the bed.

"Don't do anything careless, like get yourself killed," she said.

"I'll be back before you know it," Murphy said.

Kai set the brush aside, stood, and got into bed beside Murphy.

"You'll be back when you find that man and drag him to court at the end of the rope. That's when you'll be back," Kai said. "In the meantime, come keep me warm."

Shortly after sunup, Kai walked Boyle from the corral to the hitching post, where she placed the blanket across his back and then attached the saddle.

Michael and Aideen stood on the porch and watched.

Dressed in his black trail clothes, including hat, and with his packed saddlebags slung over his right shoulder, Murphy stepped on to the porch.

He kissed Aideen on the cheek and shook Michael's hand.

"You be careful, son," Michael said.

Murphy nodded, and then stepped down from the porch to Kai.

"I'll wire you when I can," he said and slung the saddlebags across the saddle.

191

Kai nodded. "I told you once before, I'll make you a good wife but a poor widow," she said.

"I'll remember," Murphy said.

They hugged and kissed, and then Murphy mounted the saddle and quickly rode away.

Kai went up to the steps and stood beside Michael and Aideen and watched until Murphy was out of sight.

As he ate lunch in the dining car, Murphy studied the reports on the remaining four jury members.

They were scattered to the four winds.

David Clinton in Dallas.

Donald Craig in Salt Lake City.

John Olson in Nevada.

Robert Wood in Wyoming.

By now, each was in the protective custody of the army.

By now, Stuyvesant was aware of that and would be on the move to find a safe place to regroup and plan for his future.

Stuyvesant was still young enough to wait it out, and smart enough to know protective custody only went so far over time.

If Murphy had an edge, it was that Stuyvesant was insane.

Murphy had seen many stout men suffer breakdowns during the war. Some recovered, and some occupied hospitals for the insane and would do so for the rest of their lives.

It was difficult to say what damage the war did to Stuyvesant, but no man escaped the battlefield without scars, including Murphy.

Coupled with returning home only to discover his wife's affair and that the boy he thought was his actually wasn't, in all likelihood had driven Stuyvesant to the brink.

Then, sitting in prison for twelve years finished off what was left of his sanity.

What most people failed to realize was that a person could be totally insane and brilliant at the same time.

Stuyvesant used his time in prison to hatch and perfect his revenge, while fooling all those who knew him into believing he was a sane and rational man.

There were many who believed, and Murphy was one of them, that Custer had been plagued with a touch of insanity. Murphy had witnessed some of it on the battlefield: Custer's recklessness and daring, two traits that had led to his failure at Little Bighorn.

Some said Custer's recklessness was the product of an insane mind.

Stuyvesant wasn't reckless; just the opposite. He was methodically efficient and cunning to the point of brilliance.

But still insane.

Michael rode Kai and Aideen to town in the wagon to get supplies. While the women shopped in the general store, he wandered around Fort Smith and took in the sights.

Judge Parker's courthouse was the dominant feature in the town, although the church was also an impressive structure.

Telegraph poles and lines ran down Main Street and connected to the courthouse.

When he checked his pocket watch, Michael realized he'd been wandering around for forty-five minutes, so he hurried back to the general store.

Kai and Aideen were loading the wagon when he reached them.

"And where have you been?" Aideen said.

"Just looking at the town," Michael said.

"I need to see Judge Parker," Kai said.

"Hop in. I'll ride you over to the courthouse," Michael said.

"I was afraid it would come to this," Parker said.

"Me, too," Kai said.

"His run for Congress?" Parker said.

Kai shrugged. "We don't know how long he'll be gone."

"We talked about this before, so maybe it's worth repeating," Parker said. "When Murphy returns, maybe he'll take an appointment as a US marshal in my court. He doesn't need the money, but at least he won't travel out of state."

"Mention it to him when he gets back," Kai said. "But I'm here to ask a favor. I'd like to visit the reservation tomorrow and bring Murphy's parents. I need to find out where the children left off at last spring so I can prepare for their fall lessons."

"I think that's a fine idea," Parker said. "The Indian Agent is due to make a trip to the reservation. I'll ask him to accompany you. Meet here around ten o'clock tomorrow morning."

"Thank you, Judge," Kai said.

Parker nodded. "Kai, Murphy will be all right," he said.

"I know," Kai said.

Murphy walked Boyle along the platform to where Burke stood in front of his carriage.

"He needs to run a bit," Murphy said. "I'll meet you at the White House."

Murphy mounted the saddle and rode away at a fast gallop. Burke tried his best to keep up in his carriage, but within minutes, Murphy was completely out of sight.

By the time Burke reached the White House, Murphy was walking Boyle across the lawn to the stables.

Murphy waited for Burke. Then they entered the White House and went to the Oval Office.

Murphy, Burke, Arthur, and Wise had supper in Arthur's private quarters.

"The train is ready and standing by," Arthur said. "Three engineers will make the trip. I told them to break speed records if necessary."

"Are the men ready to go?" Murphy said.

"You mean now? I figured you'd leave in the morning," Arthur said.

"Does the train have a sleeping car?" Murphy said.

"Of course," Arthur said.

"Then Agent Wise and I can sleep on the train," Murphy said.

"I'll need to get my horse," Wise said.

"Then get him, and we'll leave right after dinner," Murphy said.

"My train is at the station," Arthur said. "William, send word to the engineers that Murphy and Wise will be leaving in two hours."

Murphy looked at Wise. "Is that enough time to get your horse?"

Wise nodded.

"Then I'll meet you at the station in two hours," Murphy said.

For a few seconds, Wise didn't grasp Murphy's meaning. Then he understood and stood up. "Thank you for dinner, Mr. President," he said and left the room.

"Go easy on him, Murphy," Burke said. "He blames himself as it is."

"He should," Murphy said. "Mr. President, thank you for dinner. I think I'll see Melvin before we leave."

"His fever comes and goes," the resident doctor said. "He's regaining strength as his body mends and replaces lost blood."

"Has he woken up yet?" Murphy said.

"He's opened his eyes a few times, but that is probably a

195

Ethan J. Wolfe

reflex action," the resident doctor said. "He mumbled a few words over and over. That Stuyvesant is insane. That he could see it in his eyes."

"Thank you," Murphy said.

Just before he boarded the president's train, Murphy turned to Burke, who was there to see them off.

"Send Kai regular updates on Melvin's condition," Murphy said.

"I will," Burke said.

"Nice train," Murphy said as he took the steps and boarded the riding car.

196

CHAPTER TWENTY-SEVEN

Wise awoke shortly after six in the morning and glanced out the window of his sleeping car. The sun was new and low in the sky. He got out of bed and filled the washbasin with water.

After he washed and dressed, Wise left the car and found Murphy in the dining car, drinking coffee and smoking his pipe.

There was a large coffee pot on the stove, so Wise filled a mug and joined Murphy at the table.

"I know that you blame me for . . ." Wise said.

"I do," Murphy said.

"Not as much as I blame myself," Wise said. "If you would allow it, I'd like to explain what happened that day."

Murphy took a sip of coffee, puffed on his pipe, and nodded.

"We reached the hotel at the hot springs," Wise said. "I told the men to stay put while I went inside to check if Turner was registered. Knoop wandered off on his own. I never even knew he was gone until I came back and the shot sounded. It took us about thirty seconds to run around the springs to where Knoop was lying. We never saw who shot him, but Melvin did and said it was Stuyvesant. He was coming out of the bungalow where he had just shot Mr. Turner. Mrs. Turner was in the springs at the time. She suffers from typhoid pneumonia."

"Why didn't the rest of your team notice Knoop had wandered off?" Murphy said.

"They . . . just didn't," Wise said.

"You were the senior man. It was your responsibility to make

197

sure every man knew where every other man was at all times," Murphy said.

"I know, and I accept the blame," Wise said. "And it's a mistake I will have to live with. It's also one I won't make again."

Murphy stood up from the table. "The kitchen is well stocked, but Arthur forgot to assign a cook," he said. "I'll get breakfast going. See if the engineers are hungry."

Henry Teasel, Indian Affair's Agent, appointed by Judge Parker, met Kai, Michael, and Aideen in front of the courthouse. They took his large buggy to the reservation.

The drive took about an hour as the road outside of town took them through a pass in the mountains.

"Judge Parker has the final say on reservation matters, but the five tribes that occupy the reservation generally govern themselves," Teasel said.

"Five?" Michael said.

"The Cherokee, the Chickasaw, Choctaw, Muscogee, and Seminole," Teasel said. "I have great respect and admiration for all of them."

"When you say they govern themselves, what does that mean?" Michael said.

"They have a strict code of laws they live by, and there are harsh penalties for breaking them," Teasel said. "Theft of any sort is not tolerated. Neither is adultery. Murder is dealt with swiftly and harshly and, despite what the dime-store novels say, drunkenness is frowned upon. They hold court with tribal leaders serving as judges and counsel. Heaven help you if you make a false accusation."

Michael looked at Kai. "What will you be teaching at their school?"

"I have to review the lesson plans, but I imagine it isn't that much different from regular school lessons," Kai said. "Most, if not all, of the children speak English as well as half a dozen native languages, French, and Spanish. Some even speak Dutch. They are a very intelligent people and take pride in their intelligence."

"We're almost there," Teasel said.

At a water stop in Indiana, Murphy and Wise got off the train to stretch their legs. The countryside was lush and green, and there wasn't a house or farm in sight.

"Pretty country," Wise said.

"It is," Murphy said.

"We have a ways to go," Wise said.

"We do," Murphy said. "Another forty hours at least."

The engineers finished loading the engine car with water. "All aboard, gentlemen," an engineer said.

"I'll take a turn shoveling coal," Murphy said. "You can have kitchen duty for lunch."

While Kai met with elders inside the red brick schoolhouse, Teasel gave Michael and Aideen a tour of the gathering center on the reservation.

"I'm surprised to see so many wood buildings," Michael said.

"They harvest lumber from the mountains and have learned carpentry and blacksmithing, and there is even a butcher shop," Teasel said. "Those with the knack cowboy and raise horses to sell to the army."

"Is that a hospital?" Aideen said.

They stopped in front of a small wood structure. A wood sign over the door read *Hospital*.

"This is rather small for so large a reservation," Michael said.

"Medicine and medical professionals are lacking, above all else," Teasel said. "The red tape in Washington is usually six months behind, I'm afraid."

"Six months?" Michael said.

"That's a sad and sorry fact," Teasel said. "Even Judge Parker can't get Washington to move faster than that."

"There's Kai," Aideen said.

Walking with a tribal elder, Kai approached Michael and Aideen.

"This is Red Cloud and he is, by your years, eighty-seven years old," Kai said.

Red Cloud extended his right hand to Michael, and they shook.

"This is my wife, Aideen," Michael said.

Red Cloud shook Aideen's hand. "You married well," he said to Michael.

"I did at that," Michael said.

"Kai, what are your needs for school?" Teasel said.

"Red Cloud, while the women talk school with Mr. Teasel, why don't we find a spot in the shade and smoke our pipes?" Michael said.

"A fine idea," Red Cloud said. "I have a porch in the shade."

Michael and Red Cloud walked through the gathering center to a cabin situated alone beside a green field.

They sat on the porch and smoked their pipes.

"I have had five wives, thirteen children, and around thirty grandchildren," Red Cloud said. "My last wife died five years ago. I have been thinking of taking a sixth."

"A sixth?" Michael said. "I've had just the one, and we're going on fifty years now."

"Have you many children?" Red Cloud asked.

"One son. He's married to Kai," Michael said.

"I have heard the Irish accent spoken many time in my life, and you and your wife speak it," Red Cloud said. "You approve that your son married a woman who has Sioux blood in her veins?"

"Of course I approve," Michael said. "Kai is a smart, caring, lovely woman. She loves my son, and he loves her. That she is part Sioux doesn't matter in the least to me, my wife, or my son."

"It matters to many," Red Cloud said.

"It shouldn't," Michael said.

"No, it shouldn't," Red Cloud said. "Do you play checkers?"

"I do. Do you have coffee?"

"I do."

"Get the board."

Murphy shoveled coal for six hours so the engineers could get some rest. He took a break for dinner, ate with Wise and two engineers, and then was back at it, shoveling coal until midnight.

He took a snack of apple pie and cold milk in the kitchen and then went to bed and slept until seven.

After breakfast, he returned to shoveling coal.

He took lunch with the engineer when Wise brought them warm roast beef sandwiches and coffee.

The engineers switched out after lunch. Murphy shoveled coal until six, when he broke for dinner and joined Wise in the kitchen.

"We should reach the end of the line in about twenty hours," Murphy said. "How long a ride to the springs from that point?"

"About an hour. Less if we push it," Wise said.

"I'll shovel coal until midnight," Murphy said. "In the morning, right after breakfast, we should be at the drop-off point."

"Is that why you're shoveling coal, to kill time?" Wise asked.

"I'm shoveling coal because without it, the train won't move," Murphy said. "And yes, to kill time."

"May I ask you something?" Wise said.

"Go ahead."

"By the time we reach the hotel, it'll have been two weeks

since Stuyvesant shot Melvin. What do you hope to gain by going to the springs?" Wise said.

"By now Stuyvesant is holed up somewhere, hoping to wait it out," Murphy said. "Where he's holed up is anybody's guess. Where he shot Knoop is as good a place as any to start looking."

"You plan to track him?" Wise said. "He has a two-week head start."

"And I have the advantage of surprise," Murphy said. "I'm going back to shovel more coal. I'll see you at breakfast."

After Murphy left, Wise sat with a cup of coffee and thought for a while. He had asked around Washington, including other agents, about Murphy. Most said that Murphy was the best agent the service ever had.

One agent called Murphy the President's Regulator.

Wise asked Burke about that.

Burke told him Murphy was far more capable than most and, more important, was not afraid to do a job no one else would touch.

"Is that why Murphy is going after Stuyvesant?" Wise had asked Burke.

"No, that is why Murphy is going after Stuyvesant alone," Burke had replied.

After breakfast, Michael saddled Kai's pinto while Kai and Aideen watched from the porch.

As he led the pinto from the corral to the porch, Aideen said, "How long will you be in town?"

"Just long enough to pick up the red paint for the barn," Michael said.

Kai handed Michael an envelope. "This is a check to Mr. Grillo; could you mail it for me?"

Michael tucked the envelope into his shirt pocket, mounted

the pinto, and rode off to town. Riding the pinto at a quick gait, he reached town in less than an hour.

He dismounted at the post office and went inside to mail Kai's envelope. Then he walked the pinto to the courthouse and tied him to the hitching post reserved for visitors.

In the lobby of the courthouse, Michael asked a deputy marshal if William Teasel was in his office.

"Go down the hall to the marshal's office, and a deputy will escort you to Mr. Teasel's office," the deputy said.

Michael went to the marshal's office and a deputy escorted him to Teasel's office.

"Mr. Murphy, I wasn't expecting to see you so soon," Teasel said. "What brings you to my office?"

Michael reached into his shirt pocket and removed a folded check. "The trip to the reservation got me to thinking. I'd like to give you this check to buy medical supplies for that hospital they got there. Please don't say where you got it though."

Teasel took the check from Michael, unfolded it, and read it. "This is for ten thousand dollars," he said, shocked at the amount.

"Well, I need to buy paint for my son's barn," Michael said.

"Wait, Mr. Murphy. This is a great deal of money," Teasel said.

"Make sure you put it to good use," Michael said. "That hospital is a sorry sight."

"How? Why?" Teasel said.

"I lost at checkers," Michael said.

Murphy and Wise walked their horses down the plank at the boxcar. The engineers stood nearby and watched.

"Wait three hours for Agent Wise to return," Murphy said as he mounted. "Agent Wise, lead the way."

The ride to the hotel took less than an hour. The hotel

manager remembered Wise and allowed him and Murphy access to the grounds.

They left the horses at a hitching post near the hotel, and Wise led Murphy around the springs to the location where Knoop had been shot.

"That manager had the good sense not to rent those cabins just yet," Murphy said.

"I asked him not to," Wise said.

Murphy inspected the ground and located the tracks made by Stuyvesant as he walked to his horse.

"It's good they didn't have rain," Murphy said.

Wise looked at the dry tracks in the dirt.

"Best get back to the train now," Murphy said. "It's a long way to Washington."

"I can't go with—"

"No."

"That's plain enough," Wise said. "Can I ask you a question before I go?"

"Go ahead."

"They call you the Regulator," Wise said. "I was wondering why."

"Do you know what a Regulator is? A Regulator is a killer of men," Murphy said. "Fancy it up any way you want, but that's what it boils down to, a killer of men."

Wise looked at Murphy and then nodded.

"Goodbye Agent Murphy," Wise said.

"Safe trip, Agent Wise," Murphy said.

CHAPTER TWENTY-EIGHT

Murphy purchased forty pounds of fresh supplies from the hotel and then used their telegraph office, sending the telegrams himself.

He sent a telegram to Burke to let him know he was in Glenwood Springs and asked about Knoop's condition. He ended by writing he'd wait for a reply.

The second telegram was to Kai, telling her where he was and that he'd wire again as soon as he could.

He waited for Burke's reply, which came forty minutes later.

Knoop's condition unchanged. No longer listed as critical, but hasn't woken as yet. Keep me advised of your progress. Good luck and Godspeed.

Murphy left the hotel and walked to where Boyle was hitched. Guests in the springs and on the hotel porch stared at Murphy as he unhitched Boyle, mounted the saddle, and rode him around the springs to the rear of the cabins.

He dismounted where Stuyvesant's tracks led up a hill. He studied them closely.

"Let's walk a bit, boy," Murphy said to Boyle and took the reins.

After about an hour of climbing steep hills, the trail led down to the valley. Murphy paused, dismounted, and removed his maps from the saddlebags.

He was in the Roaring Fork Valley, where the Colorado and Roaring Fork Rivers came together.

Stuyvesant was traveling west and slightly north through the valley. Murphy took out his notes.

The Clinton Family lived in Dallas. The Woods in Wyoming. The Olsons in Nevada, and the Craigs in Salt Lake City, Utah.

West and slightly north would take a person to Salt Lake City.

Murphy used a pencil to trace the path to Salt Lake City. The distance was five hundred or more miles and much of it through the Rocky Mountains.

He put the map and notes away and rubbed Boyle's neck.

"Well, boy, we have our work cut out for us," Murphy said and mounted the saddle.

Aideen stood beside the barn and looked up at Michael, who was on a tall ladder with paintbrush and bucket in hand.

"Michael, supper is ready. Come down," Aideen said.

"There is a few minutes of light left," Michael said.

"You're not going to paint the barn in one day, Michael," Aideen said. "Come down or I'll knock the ladder down with you on it."

Michael sighed and descended the ladder.

"At least let me wash the brush and put the paint away."

"Go ahead and wash up while you're at it," Aideen said. "In fact, you'll take a bath tonight."

"Is the tub big enough for two?" Michael said.

"Still talking fresh after all these years," Aideen said.

"We're old, my dear wife, but we're not dead," Michael said. "At least not yet, anyway."

"You will be if you're not at the dinner table in fifteen minutes," Aideen said.

Aideen turned and walked toward the house, paused, and

looked back with a sly grin. "And yes, the tub is big enough for two," she said.

Close to sunset, Murphy found the site where Stuyvesant had camped the day he shot Knoop. Murphy recognized his brand of horseshoe from the tracks he left as he rode away from the hotel. All that remained of the campfire were a few scorched stones set in a circle.

Murphy built a fire inside the stones, added beans to water in a fry pan, and set them to cook while he tended to Boyle.

"We need fifty miles a day for the next ten days," Murphy said as he brushed Boyle. "So I'm going to give you a pound of grain to keep up your strength."

While Boyle ate grain from a feedbag, Murphy unwrapped fresh beef from waxed paper, cut some into strips, and added it to the fry pan.

As he waited for his supper to cook, Murphy lit his pipe and looked at Boyle.

"I know what you're thinking: why not take the railroad directly to Salt Lake City, if we're so sure that's where he's headed?" Murphy said.

Still eating grain, Boyle ignored Murphy.

Murphy stirred the beef and beans in the pan.

"Because I'm not sure," Murphy said. "Between here and there, he could have turned north or south or even east. The only way to actually be sure is to follow his trail to wherever he's going."

He stirred the pan, tested the beef, and then ladled his dinner onto a plate.

"Lucky us," Murphy said with a heavy sigh.

After a breakfast of bacon and biscuits, Murphy put the blanket and saddle on Boyle.

"Fifty miles today is our goal," he said as he mounted up. "But I'll take sixty."

By noon, Murphy found a campsite where Stuyvesant had built a fire. The distance between the two campsites was about twenty miles.

Murphy dismounted and inspected the horse tracks made in soft dirt beside the campfire pit. There was no doubt the prints were made by Stuyvesant's horse.

"He's certainly in no hurry," Murphy said as he removed the saddle from Boyle's back. "You have one hour to rest and eat your fill of grass."

He built a fire and put on a pot of coffee. When the coffee was ready, he unwrapped a loaf of cornbread and sliced off a piece.

Behind Murphy, Boyle snorted and whinnied.

"I see them, boy," Murphy said. "It's just a hunting party from the reservation."

Murphy sipped coffee and ate a piece of cornbread as he watched twelve mounted Ute Indians ride toward him. As they neared, he could see that four of the horses had freshly killed deer slung over the saddles.

All riders wore pants and boots, but were shirtless.

Murphy stayed seated when the dozen riders reached him. Only one dismounted. He was a large man, around forty years old and handsome, with chiseled features.

"I am called Bear of the Ute People," he said.

"I am called Murphy of the Irish people," Murphy said. "Sit, share some coffee and cornbread with me."

Bear sat opposite Murphy as Murphy filled an extra cup with coffee. "Sugar?"

"Yes," Bear said. "Three spoons. I like it sweet."

Murphy added three spoons of sugar from the sugar bag and sliced off a piece of cornbread for Bear.

"I see your hunting party was successful," Murphy said.

"Yes. If we see one or two more deer on the way back to the reservation, it will be even more successful," Bear said. "What are you doing out here alone in the valley?"

"I am a lawman," Murphy said. "I am hunting an outlaw who passed this way ten days ago. I believe he is on the way to Salt Lake City."

"We have seen no white man traveling alone," Bear said.

"He probably passed before you went hunting," Murphy said.

Bear nodded. "Good coffee, good cornbread."

Murphy looked at the six scars on each side of Bear's chest. "I see you have danced the Sun Dance many times," he said.

Bear looked his question at Murphy.

"My wife is part Navajo," Murphy said. "She has danced the dance herself."

Bear nodded. "Are you a good tracker?"

"Fair, if the signs are good," Murphy said.

Bear stood up and spoke to his men in his native Ute language. They turned their horses and rode away.

Bear looked at Murphy. "I will track with you for a while," he said. "If you don't mind the company."

"So what did this man do that you are hunting him through the valley?" Bear said as he and Murphy rode west.

"He killed eight men in cold blood, and he's looking to make it thirteen," Murphy said.

"Did they wrong him in some way?"

"He thinks so," Murphy said. "After the war he murdered his wife for taking a lover while he was away. A jury of twelve men found him guilty of murdering his wife and her lover, and he spent a dozen years in prison. When he got out, he started hunting and killing the twelve members of the jury that sent him to prison."

"I understand," Bear said. "The word of our tribal council is final, like your judge. To disobey the word means banishment or death."

"It's pretty much the same thing with our system in the courts," Murphy said.

"If you catch this man, will you kill him?"

"If I take him alive, he will be judged in court and will probably hang for his crimes."

"Hanging is a bad way to leave this world," Bear said.

"Yes, it is," Murphy said. "But, he could be found insane and spend the rest of his life in a prison hospital."

"Insane?" Bear said.

"*Loco*," Murphy said.

"So if a man is found *loco*, he doesn't pay for his crimes?" Bear said.

"Spending all of your remaining days in a prison hospital without ever seeing the light of day, to some, is worse than being hanged," Murphy said.

"Our people are not so different," Bear said.

"Not really," Murphy said. "I have worked and lived with whites, blacks, Chinese, and Indians, and I can't really tell the difference. Language, sure; culture, sure; but inside we're all the same, as far as I can see."

Bear nodded. "There was a time in my youth when I would have killed any white man on sight just because he was white," he said.

Murphy grinned. "Then I'm glad we didn't meet when we were young."

Bear looked at Murphy and nodded. "How did you come to take a Navajo wife?"

"A few years back I was working another case, chasing another outlaw. That case took me to Fort Smith in Arkansas," Murphy said. "Kai owned a boarding house where I stayed. We just sort of hit it off and, the next thing I know, we were married."

"Has she given you sons?"

"Not yet, but we're working on it."

"It's hard to work on it when you are here and she is there."

Murphy grinned again. "It is that," he said.

"I see a campsite up ahead," Bear said.

"It's his," Murphy said. "I recognize his horse's tracks."

"It's a good spot to camp for tonight," Bear said.

"Might as well, as there's only an hour of daylight left," Murphy said.

Burke was in his office when a messenger arrived with a message from Saint Elizabeth's Hospital.

Knoop was awake and had asked for him.

After sunset, Murphy dished out two plates of food and coffee. The meal consisted of beans, strips of beef, and cornbread.

"The man you hunt, why is he going to the Salt Lake?" Bear said.

"One of the men he wants to kill has moved there," Murphy said. "By now the local authorities have taken him into protective custody. The only way I'm going to know where the man I'm after is going next is to follow him."

"He is a determined man," Bear said.

"So am I," Murphy said.

"We thought we'd lost you for a while," Burke said.

Knoop was sitting up in bed, propped against several pillows.

"Where is Murphy? I have to talk to him," Knoop said.

"He went after Stuyvesant," Burke said. "I honestly don't know where he is at the moment."

"I looked into Stuyvesant's eyes," Knoop said. "The man is

completely insane."

"Melvin, please relax," Burke said. "If ever a man could take care of himself, it's Murphy. Right now, you have to rest and get your strength back."

"I need to get out of this hospital," Knoop said.

"And do what, in your condition?" Burke said.

Knoop sat back and sighed.

"Exactly," Burke said.

"I will ride with you one more day," Bear said.

"Glad to have the company," Murphy said. "Conversations with my horse can be a bit one-sided."

Murphy emptied the coffee pot into two cups, added sugar, and gave one cup to Bear.

"Why are you called Bear?" Murphy said.

"When I was a boy of ten in the land you now call Utah, my father traded ponies with a trader for a Hawken rifle," Bear said. "Do you know this weapon?"

"I owned one for a very long time," Murphy said.

"We went hunting for mule deer in the mountains," Bear said. "My father was attacked by a black bear and the bear killed him. I shot the bear with the Hawken and killed the bear. The elders called me Bear to remember the good death of my father."

"You have been to the Salt Lake?" Murphy said.

"Many times as a boy," Bear said. "Before the Mormons came and built their city. The state is named after the Ute People, but all anybody knows of Utah is the Mormons and mountain saltwater."

In the distance a wolf howled. Its piercing cry echoed for several seconds.

"It sounds like someone made a kill," Bear said.

Boyle and Bear's horses nervously whinnied.

"We'll keep a fire going tonight and hobble our horses closer,"

Murphy said.

Bear removed his Winchester rifle from the saddle sleeve and placed it within his arm's length.

Murphy tossed extra sticks and wood on the fire and then leaned against his saddle and lit his pipe.

"No offense, but the only thing that could make a night like this better is if my wife was here instead of you," Murphy said.

Bear looked at Murphy. "No offense taken," he said.

"Send this telegram right away, priority status," Burke told the White House operator.

The operator read the text and said, "Will you be waiting for a reply?"

"I doubt one will be coming until tomorrow," Burke said.

"Good night then, sir," the operator said.

"Good night," Burke said.

"How far will you ride with me tomorrow?" Murphy said.

"Until dark. Then, in the morning, I will leave you," Bear said.

"If I forget to say it tomorrow, you've been fine company," Murphy said.

"And you have been a fine cook," Bear said with a sly grin.

CHAPTER TWENTY-NINE

Riding side by side, Murphy and Bear paused when they spotted black dots circling overhead in the distance.

Murphy removed binoculars from a saddlebag and zoomed in on the dots, which were a flock of turkey vultures.

"Turkey buzzards, and you can bet there is a bunch more of them feasting on the ground," Murphy said.

Bear dismounted and inspected the tracks they were following. "His horse has gone lame," he said. "The right rear leg is bad."

"Now we know what the buzzards are feasting on," Murphy said.

Bear mounted his horse, and he and Murphy rode a half mile west to where dozens of buzzards were eating what was left of Stuyvesant's horse.

"He took his supplies and left the saddle," Murphy said.

On the saddle was an empty sleeve for a rifle, so Stuyvesant was armed with more than just a .36 caliber Navy Colt.

"Let's see how far he got on foot," Murphy said.

They rode for three hours and, in early afternoon, they spotted another group of buzzards flying overhead.

When they reached the buzzards, they were picking at the bones of two dead adults and three children. The remains lay beside a covered wagon.

Murphy and Bear dismounted and chased the buzzards away.

"He murdered an entire family just to get their horse," Murphy said.

"Don't the wagons have two horses?" Bear said.

"I don't see a second horse, so it must have run off," Murphy said.

"Tracks head south from here," Bear said.

"There must have been saddles in the wagon," Murphy said.

Murphy checked the wagon and found one saddle. Most of the supplies were gone. As he rummaged through the dead family's personal belongings, he found a Mormon Bible.

"This is why they were traveling through the valley," he said and showed the Bible to Bear. "Mormons on the way to Salt Lake City."

"He killed them all when he could have taken one horse," Bear said. "Even during the great wars between our peoples, I would not have done such a thing."

"I saw some shovels in the wagon. Let's bury the remains," Murphy said.

Michael sat in the wagon and waited for Kai and Aideen. When they finally arrived from the house, they were dressed nearly alike in blue skirts and white blouses.

"Who is who?" Michael said.

As they stepped up into the seat, Aideen said, "You're married to the old one."

As they reached the midpoint of the ride to town, a telegraph express rider flagged them down.

"Are you Mrs. Murphy?" he said.

"They both are," Michael said. "Which one do you want?"

"It doesn't say. It just says Mrs. Murphy, Fort Smith."

"I'll take them," Kai said.

The rider handed Kai two envelopes, turned, and rode back to town.

Kai opened one and read it quickly. "My husband is in Glenwood Springs and will telegram again as soon as he can."

Kai opened the second telegram, read it quickly, and said, "It's from Mr. Burke. Melvin is awake and asked for me."

Michael turned the wagon around and Aideen said, "What are you doing?"

"Kai is going to want to pack for her trip to Washington," Michael said.

After burying the remains of the five bodies, Murphy and Bear made camp beside the wagon. There was a large, covered water barrel in the wagon, and each man used the ladle to pour water over their hair and faces.

"You will follow him south?" Bear said as they waited for supper to cook.

"No choice," Murphy said.

"Why do you think he decided not to go to the Salt Lake?" Bear said.

"I suspect it's this," Murphy said. He showed Bear the newspaper he found in the wagon beside the Bible. Stuyvesant's picture was above the story. "It's a story about him, 'The Ghost Shooter,' and how the remaining families of the jury will be under protection of the government. He read this, probably after he killed the Mormons, and decided to head south."

"To where?"

"I don't know," Murphy said. "But I do know that if he's killing strangers, he's gone completely insane."

"I don't know much of your justice in your court," Bear said. "But I do know this man won't be taken alive if he can help it."

"I suspect you are right," Murphy said.

As the train conductor called for boarding, Michael kissed Aideen and then hugged Kai.

"I should be going with you," Michael said.

"Somebody has to take care of the horses. Besides, you haven't finished painting the barn," Aideen said.

"I survived being captured by the Sioux and the Civil War in my backyard. A short train ride isn't going to kill us," Kai said.

"I expect not," Michael said.

"See you in a day or two, dear," Aideen said.

"And don't forget to send the telegram to Mr. Burke," Kai said.

Murphy and Bear rested their backs against their saddles, drank coffee, and watched stars slowly emerge as the sky darkened.

Murphy lit his pipe and quietly puffed.

"Have you killed many men, Murphy?" Bear said.

"Too many," Murphy said. "First in the war, and then as a lawman."

"I too have killed many," Bear said. "But it's an odd thing. I realized not long ago that most of the men I have killed were my own kind in tribal wars. I searched my memory for the white men I killed and could not think of but one or two."

"In the Civil War, all the men I killed were my own kind. I guess you could say the same for all the outlaws I've killed, as well," Murphy said.

Bear looked at Murphy. "It is good those days are behind us," he said.

Murphy nodded. "Would you care for more coffee?"

"Please," Bear said. "And maybe a piece of that cornbread."

Burke was waiting for Kai and Aideen at the station when the train arrived at ten o'clock at night.

"Nice to see you both again," Burke said. "I reserved a hotel room for you near the hospital."

"Take us to Melvin," Kai said as she climbed into Burke's carriage.

"But the hospital has—" Burke said.

"Aideen, are you coming?" Kai said.

Aideen climbed aboard beside Kai.

Burke said. "Hospital it is," he said.

"I have to find Murphy and warn him about Stuyvesant," Knoop said.

"Nonsense, Melvin," Kai said. "I've spoken to the doctor, and he said you need at least a month of rest before that wound is completely healed. He said if you go bouncing around, it could open up, and you could hemorrhage to death from internal bleeding."

"But Murphy is—" Knoop said.

"The most capable man I have ever known. The only thing you would do in your condition is slow him down," Kai said. "In the morning, you're coming with us to Fort Smith, where you'll rest and recover for the next month."

Knoop looked at Burke.

"Doctor's orders," Burke said.

CHAPTER THIRTY

After breakfast, Murphy and Bear saddled their horses.

Before mounting the saddle, Murphy said, "Have you ever heard the word *ballistics*?"

"No," Bear said as he shook his head.

"Each gun, long or short, makes its own mark," Murphy said, "on the bullet. There are no two guns that make the same mark."

Murphy drew his Colt and fired a shot into the dirt.

"Now fire your Winchester," Murphy said.

Bear fired a shot into the dirt.

Murphy dug out the bullets and showed them to Bear. "This is the mark made by your Winchester, and this is the mark made by my Colt," he said. "I will keep your bullet as a reminder of what a fine traveling companion you are."

Bear nodded. "And I shall keep yours," he said.

"Travel well," Murphy said and mounted the saddle.

"You, too, Murphy," Bear said.

Bear mounted his horse and he rode east while Murphy traveled south.

Stuyvesant was traveling south and slightly east to avoid the higher altitude of the Rocky Mountains.

That told Murphy nothing about Stuyvesant's destination, if he even had one. For all Murphy knew, Stuyvesant was now wandering aimlessly after reading the story in the newspaper back at the Mormon's wagon.

Late in the afternoon, Murphy found the campsite where Stuyvesant had spent the night. He checked the horse prints carefully. There was no doubt Stuyvesant was riding the Mormon's horse.

After building a fire, Murphy gave Boyle a thorough grooming and fed him a pound of grain.

While beans and bacon cooked in the pan, Murphy dug out his maps and studied the area.

It was a sure thing that Stuyvesant would avoid towns, now that he knew the extent of his exposure in the press. He couldn't risk some local lawman recognizing him from the news story, and maybe even a wanted poster by now.

Still, Stuyvesant would need supplies. He could hunt, but gunshots might attract unwanted attention.

Would he risk visiting a town?

Murphy studied the map again and then looked at Boyle. "It's possible," he said.

Michael was waiting with the wagon when the train arrived from Fort Smith. Kai, Aideen, and Knoop got off along with dozens of other passengers and walked to him.

"Hello, Melvin," Michael said.

"Hello, sir," Knoop said.

"How are you feeling?"

"A bit tired and a bit sore."

"Well, since we have an hour's ride home I stopped by Delmonico's and reserved us a table for dinner," Michael said.

"Excellent idea, Michael," Aideen said.

Michael helped Aideen and Kai into the rear seats of the wagon, and then he and Knoop got up front.

"Steaks are a waiting," Michael said.

★ ★ ★ ★ ★

Burke carried the bad news to President Arthur a few minutes after he received the telegram.

"Another copycat shooting happened in Boston this afternoon," Burke said and showed the telegram to Arthur.

"The remaining families?" Arthur said.

"In protective custody, but it no longer matters if others are copying what Stuyvesant started," Burke said.

"What did the stock market close at today?" Arthur said.

"Down another one hundred and fifty points."

Arthur sighed loudly. "There is only one way to end this and regain the public trust," he said. "A public hanging, with reporters from across the country to make the statement that lawless behavior will not be tolerated in America."

"New York City would never agree to that," Burke said. "Not even by executive order."

"Suggestions?"

"Remember the kidnapping case Murphy handled?" Burke said. "We moved the trial and execution to Fort Smith and Judge Parker's jurisdiction."

"Yes, of course," Arthur said. "Fort Smith is the perfect place for this bastard to hang in public, provided Murphy brings him back alive."

"The next time Murphy telegraphs, I'll instruct an immediate reply with instructions to bring Stuyvesant in alive to Washington for arraignment," Burke said.

"Not New York?"

"Stuyvesant has killed outside of New York. That makes it a federal case," Burke said. "We can arraign him here and try him in Fort Smith."

Arthur nodded. "Better contact Judge Parker."

"I'll go in person," Burke said.

★ ★ ★ ★ ★

Knoop sat on the front porch and watched the stars. He thought everybody was asleep, but the screen door suddenly opened and Kai came out, holding two glasses of milk, and took the chair next to him. She gave him one glass.

"Are you in pain?" Kai said. "Do you want some of the medicine the doctor gave you for pain?"

"I'm not in any pain," Knoop said and sipped milk.

"And yet here you sit after midnight, when you should be resting," Kai said.

"I've let Murphy down," Knoop said. "Betrayed the trust he placed in me as an agent of the Secret Service."

"You've done no such thing," Kai said.

"If I wasn't so inexperienced and stupid, I would have stayed with the other agents," Knoop said. "We had more than enough men to capture Stuyvesant, but because I wandered off on my own and allowed myself to get shot, he got away. And now Murphy is out there somewhere chasing after him when he should be here at home with you."

"Melvin, don't think for one second I'm not aware of who and what my husband is," Kai said. "But that's not the reason he chose you for the Secret Service. He sees in you the same intelligence and ability for rational thought that he sees in himself. Nobody expects you to be a gunman, least of all my husband. What he does expect is for you to use your talents as an investigator to your fullest potential."

Knoop sighed and sipped some milk.

"I wonder where he is," Knoop said.

"Heaven knows, but where he is, it's by his choice and mine," Kai said.

"Yours?"

"I insisted he go," Kai said. "As much as I'd rather he be home with me right now, I understand and accept that he does

222

have a strong sense of duty. Sometimes it's best to just step out of the way and let him do his job."

"I thought you'd be mad at me," Knoop said.

"Don't be foolish," Kai said. "Now finish that milk and get some rest."

CHAPTER THIRTY-ONE

Stuyvesant was staying clear of the mountains as he continued to travel south through the foothills.

Murphy broke camp at dawn and rode thirty miles by early afternoon. He stopped to rest Boyle for an hour and ate a cold lunch of cornbread and water while Boyle ate his fill of tall, sweet grass.

Murphy knew the country, having traveled this way a few years back when he was tracking a vicious killer named John Quad.

Quad's sister, Reeva, and her husband ran a large general store that supplied ranchers, farmers, and travelers. Quad had stopped there for supplies, and so did Murphy.

Quad would not be taken alive and Murphy had been forced to kill him. Afterward, Murphy took Quad's body to be buried on the Quad family farm in Ohio.

Soon after that, Murphy wrote Quad's sister a detailed letter of her brother's death.

Once Boyle was rested, Murphy rubbed his neck. "I need twenty more miles, boy," he said.

The painted sign had been replaced with a professionally made one that read, *Bensen's General Store and Mercantile.*

Otherwise, the large storefront with a home in the rear was unchanged. It was the close of the business day, and only a few customers remained when Murphy dismounted and tied Boyle to a hitching post.

Reeva Bensen stood behind the counter, waiting on a final customer when Murphy entered the store. She recognized Murphy upon sight.

"Jorgen," she said loud enough for her husband to hear from another part of the store.

Jorgen Bensen, white apron around his waist, appeared from another room and looked at Murphy.

"Set another plate at the dinner table," Reeva said. "We have a guest."

"My son, Jorgen Junior, and my daughters, Mary and Kathleen," Reeva said. "Do you remember Mr. Murphy?"

The boy and his sisters nodded.

They were at the dinner table in the living quarters behind the store.

"Please don't be shy, Mr. Murphy. Dig right in," Reeva said.

"That was quite an elegant letter you wrote a while back," Jorgen said.

"I know you had to do your duty, and I'm grateful that you buried my brother on the family farm," Reeva said. "I took some time off from the store and visited the farm in Ohio. My brother would be pleased to know he is resting beside his family and our parents."

"It was the least I could do," Murphy said.

"So, are you just passing through, or are you here on business?" Jorgen said.

"Maybe we should talk about that after dinner and let Mr. Murphy eat in peace," Reeva said.

Taking coffee on the front porch, Murphy showed Reeva and Jorgen the photograph of Stuyvesant.

"He's grown his hair and beard since this picture, but I

believe he stopped here for supplies," Murphy said. "He carries an old cap-and-ball Navy Colt and a rifle, probably a Winchester."

"Seven, maybe eight days ago, he stopped by for supplies," Reeva said. "Bought a hundred pounds of food and paid with two twenty-dollar gold pieces."

"Did he say anything, like where he was headed?" Murphy said.

"No. He just handed me a list at the counter and then waited outside on the porch," Reeva said.

"I thought he was a bit odd and watched him through the window," Jorgen said. "He kept looking off in the distance as if he expected somebody to come riding after him."

"I guess somebody was," Reeva said.

"When he left, which way did he ride?" Murphy said.

"South, due east a bit," Jorgen said.

"Mr. Murphy, you're not going now," Reeva said. "We have an extra room not in use, and you can get a fresh start after breakfast."

"I'll put your horse in our barn for the night," Jorgen said.

"I'd best do that," Murphy said. "Boyle is a bit testy around strangers."

"Mr. Burke, what brings you to my courthouse?" Judge Parker said when Burke was escorted by a deputy into Parker's chambers.

"A request from the president," Burke said.

"Oh?"

"Murphy is out tracking Stuyvesant, as you know," Burke said. "If he brings him in alive, the president would like him tried in your court."

"Hanged in my court, is what you mean," Parker said.

"With great fanfare to discourage others from doing what

he's doing," Burke said.

"If Murphy brings him back alive, which he probably won't," Parker said.

"It was made clear to him that alive is preferable," Burke said.

"But was it made clear to Stuyvesant?" Parker said.

"That I can't answer," Burke said.

Parker nodded. "Will you be staying in town long?"

"Long enough to see Kai and Melvin," Burke said. "I'll stop by for a drink later."

Burke, Kai, and Melvin sat in chairs on the porch after lunch. Each had a cup of coffee.

"This is a fine house you have here, Kai," Burke said.

Kai nodded. "Have you had any recent news of my husband?"

"Last I heard, he'd left Glenwood Springs," Burke said.

"Since then?" Kai said.

"Nothing yet," Burke said.

Aideen opened the screen door and stepped out with a cup and the coffee pot. She set the pot on the table and sat beside Knoop.

"Michael wants to stop by the general store for some hardware for the barn. He can check the post office and telegraph office while he's there," Aideen said.

"Maybe I'll go with him," Knoop said.

Kai glared at Knoop.

"A carriage ride isn't going to hurt me," Knoop said. "I feel better and stronger every day."

"Michael will watch him," Aideen said.

Michael arrived from the barn in the wagon. "I won't be long," he said.

Knoop stood up. "I'm going with you."

"Glad to have the company," Michael said.

"You watch the gopher holes," Aideen said.

After breakfast, Murphy purchased one hundred pounds of supplies, including twenty pounds of grain for Boyle.

Reeva insisted on Murphy not paying, since he'd paid for her brother's burial and headstone.

Murphy asked her son to help him load the supplies onto the saddlebags. He gave the boy forty dollars and told him to quietly give it to his father when his mother wasn't around.

Murphy easily picked up Stuyvesant's trail, despite the heavy traffic to and from the Bensen's general store, as most folks used wagons.

By midday, Stuyvesant's trail turned slightly east, away from the foothills and toward prairie ground.

Over a cold lunch of canned fruit, cornbread, and water, Murphy studied his maps. The closest major town was Gunnison, about eighty miles south and slightly east.

Stuyvesant had supplies for a long ride, so he wouldn't stop at Gunnison to resupply. He could probably make it all the way to Alamosa before he needed to stop before crossing the Rio Grande.

If that was his destination.

The truth was Murphy had no idea where Stuyvesant was headed, and maybe neither did Stuyvesant.

It was entirely possible, now that he knew the remaining jury members were out of his reach and that he was a wanted man by name and photograph, Stuyvesant had no plan at all.

Stuyvesant was the worst kind of outlaw to pursue.

He had nothing to gain and nothing to lose.

Life had little to no meaning for him.

And he was most likely insane.

Murphy stood and saddled Boyle.

"We have some ground to cover before dark," Murphy said.
Boyle snorted as Murphy mounted the saddle.

Michael exited the post office with several pieces of mail for
Kai. Knoop was waiting in the wagon. After Michael got beside
him, Michael said, "I got the supplies, and I got the mail. Let's
head back before the women think we have girlfriends."

The ride to the house took about an hour. Kai and Aideen
were on the porch, shucking corn.

"Bring those letters to Kai while I put the wagon in the barn,"
Michael said.

Knoop took the letters up to the porch and gave them to Kai.

The first letter was from Mr. Grillo, thanking them for the
check Kai had sent for the barn.

The second letter was from the adoption agency.

Kai stood up. "Melvin, tell Michael to leave the wagon
hitched. Hurry."

Burke was coming out of the telegraph office after sending a
message to the president when Kai, Aideen, Knoop, and Michael arrived in the wagon.

"Kai, is something wrong?" Burke said.

"No," Kai said as she jumped down from the wagon and
raced up the steps. She paused and said, "Have you had dinner
yet?"

"No, I was—" Burke said.

"Wait for me here. We'll all have dinner together," Kai said
and rushed into the telegraph office.

Burke stepped down to the wagon. "What is this all about?"

"A baby," Aideen said. "The agency in Little Rock approved
them for adoption, and they have a six-month-old baby girl who
needs a home."

★ ★ ★ ★ ★

Late in the afternoon, Murphy studied Stuyvesant's tracks and determined that he had turned slightly west. He had made a circle out of stones and camped for the night. Murphy took advantage of the stones and built a fire for his own supper.

While Boyle ate a pound of grain, Murphy brushed and groomed him until his thick, black coat had a shine to it.

As he waited for his supper to cook, Murphy studied his options.

He could continue to follow Stuyvesant to wherever it was he was going.

Or he could ride to Gunnison, telegraph Burke and Kai, and hope to pick up his trail at a later date.

The only answer was to pick up the pace and hope to catch up to Stuyvesant before he disappeared entirely.

Telegrams would just have to wait.

"Michael, Aideen, and I are perfectly capable of taking a two-hour train ride to Little Rock on our own," Kai said.

"At least take Melvin with you," Michael said. "It's not right for unescorted women to travel alone on a train."

"Said who?" Aideen said.

"I'd be happy to go with you," Knoop said.

"So would I," Burke said.

Kai looked at Burke.

"Murphy is my friend, and Michael is correct. Unescorted women shouldn't travel alone on a train, especially if one is carrying a baby," Burke said.

"We should all go," Michael said. "It's only a two-hour train ride."

The waiter came to the table to clear the dirty dishes.

"Would anyone care for coffee?" he said.

★ ★ ★ ★ ★

As he drank a cup of coffee, Murphy studied his maps. With some hard riding, he could be in New Mexico in three days.

That meant, if he didn't change direction, Stuyvesant was already a quarter south into New Mexico. In a week, he could be across the border into Mexico where he could disappear forever.

That had to be his destination.

Old Mexico.

And to get to Mexico, you had to cross a very large desert.

CHAPTER THIRTY-TWO

The administrator of the orphanage in Little Rock, Mrs. Bainbridge, looked across her desk at Kai and Aideen.

"It's only been three months since I've taken over as administrator, but if I had to guess as to which Mrs. Murphy filed the adoption papers I would say . . ."

"Me," Kai said. "Aideen is my mother-in-law. My husband is away on a business trip at the moment."

"I see," Mrs. Bainbridge said. "Well, would you like to know about the baby?"

"Of course," Kai said. "That's why we're here."

"She is six months old and half English and half Abenaki," Mrs. Bloomberg said. "The father is English. He is a scout for the army. Her mother died shortly after delivery of complications. The father realized he is in no position to raise a child and contacted us to place the child up for adoption."

"May we see her?" Kai said.

"That's why I'm here," Mrs. Bainbridge said. "I'll have her brought in from the nursery."

Mrs. Bainbridge left the office for a few moments and then returned to her desk.

"There is final paperwork to complete, so we might as well . . ." she said as the door opened and a nurse entered with the baby wrapped in a blanket.

"Mrs. Murphy?" the nurse said.

Kai slowly stood up and looked at the baby in the nurse's arms.

At noon, Murphy dismounted and inspected Stuyvesant's tracks.

"We're closing ground, Boyle," he said. "You're a far better mount than the one he is riding."

Murphy returned to the saddle and followed Stuyvesant's tracks until, about an hour later, a bullet grazed his forehead, a shot rang out, and he fell from the saddle.

Murphy rolled, drew his Colt, rolled onto his stomach, and lay still. Boyle walked to him and nuzzled Murphy's shoulder.

"Back away, boy. You know the drill," Murphy whispered.

Boyle backed away from Murphy and found some grass to munch on.

Murphy didn't move and kept his breathing as shallow as possible. A full minute or more passed before he heard three men approaching. One of the men wore spurs.

"Fine-looking mount," one of the men said.

"Get his money, watch, and boots," another man said. "Then we go through his supplies."

"Turn him over," a third said.

As soon as a hand touched Murphy, he rolled and shot the man in the face.

Boyle reared up and smashed a second man in the back of the head, cracking it open like an egg.

The third man reached for his sidearm, but Murphy jumped to his feet, cocked the Colt, and stuck it into the man's belly.

"You bushwhacking piece of trash," Murphy said. "Blink, and see what happens to your insides."

"Please, mister. I didn't shoot you. It wasn't me, I swear it," the man said. "Don't kill me, please."

"No, you were just going to rob me and steal my horse," Murphy said.

"Only 'cause I thought you was dead," the man said. "But I didn't shoot. Check my sidearm. You'll see."

"I'm going to ask you once, and if I don't like your answer, I'll send you to where your friends are," Murphy said. "Did you see a man riding alone? Long hair, beard, riding south."

"No. We was coming west," the man said. "All we saw was you."

Murphy stared at the man, whose eyes were like those of a frightened rabbit.

"Honest, mister, we was just trying to get through the territory," the man said.

"By ambushing strangers?" Murphy said. "There's a shovel in my saddle. Bury your friends."

"Bury them? What fer? Buzzards gotta eat too, you know," the man said.

"You know, you're right," Murphy said. "Start walking. Leave your sidearm here and start walking."

"Walk? Where?"

"North," Murphy said. "For two hours. Then turn around and come back for your horse."

"But—"

"Leave your gun and start walking, or you can start dying," Murphy said.

The man dropped his sidearm. "The horses are just over that little hill yonder," he said.

"Go, and consider this your lucky day," Murphy said.

"You're a hard man, mister," the man said. "I'll see you again."

"You better hope not, or I'll be the last thing you ever see before you meet your maker."

The man walked away, heading north.

Murphy picked up the man's gun and the guns of the dead men and tucked them into a saddlebag, then mounted the saddle and rode to the hill where three horses were tethered to a tree.

Murphy dismounted, took the rifles from the saddles, and then used his rope to link the three horses together.

He opened a saddlebag on Boyle and removed a bottle of his father's bourbon and a clean bandana. He poured some bourbon on the bandana and wiped the cut on his forehead.

Then he mounted up and led the three horses for several miles south and then set them free.

Kai held the baby girl in her arms as the train slowly left the station in Little Rock. Aideen sat next to her while Burke, Michael, and Knoop sat in the seats opposite her.

"She's a beautiful baby," Burke said.

"She is that," Michael said.

"What about a name?" Knoop said.

"Yes, she'll need a proper name," Michael said.

"I think I'll wait until Murphy returns, so we can name her together," Kai said.

"May I hold her for a while?" Aideen said.

Kai handed the baby to Aideen.

"Melvin, could you take my bag to the dining car and have the bottles filled with warm milk," Kai said.

Michael said, "I'll go with you."

"If you ladies can manage without me, I believe I will also go so I can smoke a cigar," Burke said.

Once the men were gone, Aideen said, "I do believe the men abandoned ship just in time. She needs to be changed."

Close to sundown, Murphy made camp. After tending to Boyle, he built a fire and studied his maps.

He was just a day and a half from the border of New Mexico Territory.

If Stuyvesant stayed on his present course, he would reach the desert in New Mexico. After that, he could cross the border and be lost forever.

Even though Boyle was making up ten miles a day on Stuyvesant, it wasn't enough to catch him before he reached the desert.

Murphy studied his options.

He could continue his pursuit of Stuyvesant. If Stuyvesant reached the border of Mexico, he was gone for good.

Murphy could ride to the nearest town with a telegraph office, wire the governor, and request marshals be sent out to cover the border.

If he did that, he might not pick up the trail again.

Murphy put the maps away, filled a plate with beans and bacon, and cut off a piece of cornbread.

He looked at Boyle. "We'll follow," he said. "For now."

Kai sat in the rocking chair on the porch and fed the baby a bottle of warm milk. Aideen, Michael, Knoop, and Burke also sat in chairs and watched.

"Tomorrow I'll go to town and buy a crib, clothes, a supply of bottles and diapers, and anything else we'll need," Kai said.

"I have to return to Washington in the morning," Burke said. "So I'll hitch a ride with you to town."

Kai looked at Burke. "Find my husband, Mr. Burke. Wherever he is, you find him and tell him to come home. Tell him he has a daughter, and he needs to come home."

CHAPTER THIRTY-THREE

"Still no word from Murphy?" Arthur said.

"No, but that isn't all that unusual," Burke said. "He is probably in pursuit and unable to access a telegraph office."

"Hell, man, have you seen the papers today?" Arthur said. "The stock market is down another three hundred points, and there has been another copycat shooting in Texas. Find Murphy, and then find out what the hell is going on. And I mean today."

Thirty miles from the border of New Mexico, Stuyvesant made a sudden swing to the east. Murphy dismounted and inspected the tracks carefully so there would be no mistake.

There wasn't.

Murphy rubbed Boyle's long, muscular neck. "I need another ten miles before we can rest tonight," he said.

He mounted the saddle and rode Boyle at a medium pace until thirty minutes before sunset. He searched for a campsite and found a circle of rocks where Stuyvesant had made camp.

The odd thing was that the ashes in the firepit were enough for a half-dozen fires and were only three days old, when they should be at least six.

"Stay put for a few minutes, boy," Murphy said.

He followed the tracks leading away from the firepit for several hundred feet. There was no doubt the horse was the same horse Stuyvesant had stolen from the Mormons.

The horse showed no signs of going lame, so why the long stopover in the middle of nowhere?

Murphy returned to the campsite, gathered up wood and tumbleweed, and built a fire. As supper cooked, he brushed and groomed Boyle.

"I'm tired, boy," Murphy said as he ran the brush across Boyle's thick back. "Tired and sick of this life of hunting outlaws for a bunch of thankless politicians."

Boyle turned his neck and looked at Murphy. "I know I promised you a comfortable retirement, but we have to finish this last job first."

When the food was ready, Murphy filled a plate and sat with his back against the saddle.

"Why did he stay three days and nights in this one spot?" he said aloud.

Boyle turned and looked at Murphy.

Murphy looked at Boyle.

"His horse could have had a sore leg and needed the rest, but his tracks show no signs of that," Murphy said. "Or . . . he stopped to figure out what he was going to do next."

In response to Murphy's voice, Boyle snorted.

"I agree. His plans went to hell when Knoop showed up in Glenwood," Murphy said. "He finally put it all together and realized he has nowhere to go."

Boyle snorted again.

"Right," Murphy said. "So where is he going?"

"That's all of them. That's every US marshal in the country," the White House telegraph operator said. "And the Texas Rangers in Austin."

"Have a second operator stand by for replies, and get started on the county sheriffs," Burke said.

"All of them?"

"Yes, all of them," Burke said. "I'll be in my office all night."

Shortly after midnight, Kai sat in the rocking chair on the front porch and fed the baby a bottle of infant formula she bought at the general store in town.

She had lit the wall lantern so she could see the baby clearly. In the soft, glowing light, the girl was absolutely beautiful.

"Well, my nameless little daughter, when you grow up, you will know both sides of your heritage and be proud of each," she said.

The screen door opened and Aideen stepped out. "I thought I heard you get up," she said and sat beside Kai.

"Midnight feeding," Kai said.

"I'll take the two o'clock, so you can get some sleep," Aideen said.

The screen door opened again and Michael stepped out. "Is something wrong? Is the baby sick?"

"No dear, just hungry," Aideen said.

Michael sat next to Aideen as the screen door opened a third time, and Knoop stepped out onto the porch.

"The midnight feeding," Knoop said as he took a chair. "I can take the two a.m."

"You know about babies?" Kai said, surprised.

"When I was twelve, my mother gave birth to a baby girl. After my mother became very ill, I did the feeding, the changing, and bathing while my father worked the farm back in Scotland," Knoop said. "And she's done and ready to be burped."

Kai handed the baby and shoulder blanket to Knoop and he delicately, expertly burped the baby.

"You relax, and I'll put her to bed," Knoop said.

After Knoop took the baby into the house, Kai shook her head. "Wonders never cease," she said.

Burke, asleep on the sofa in his office, opened his eyes when there was a knock on the door.

He sat up. "Come," he said.

The door opened and a telegraph operator carrying an oil lamp stepped in.

"Mr. Burke, we got this from the county sheriff in Arapahoe County in Colorado," he said.

Burke went to his desk and lit the oil lamp.

"What does he say?" Burke said.

"He and some deputies were transporting some prisoners to Denver when they spotted a man in the distance who could be Mr. Murphy," the operator said.

"Could be?" Burke said.

Burke sat, opened a desk drawer, and removed a large map. "Arapahoe County is about forty miles east of the Rockies," he said. "At the base is a general store called Bensen's, used by locals, traders, and trappers. Send this sheriff a telegram and ask him to take a ride to Bensen's and speak with Reeva Bensen. Have him ask her if Murphy stopped by."

"Right now?"

"Yes, right now," Burke said.

After the operator left, Burke opened a desk drawer, produced a bottle of bourbon, and poured a drink. He took a sip and looked at the map. "What the hell are you doing in Denver?" he said aloud.

Murphy awoke an hour before sunrise. He built a fire, put on a pot of coffee, and then fed Boyle a pound of grain.

For breakfast, Murphy ate a few hard biscuits with coffee and was in the saddle by sunrise.

Stuyvesant's trail moved southeast toward the Rio Grande River.

Around noon, Murphy dismounted to give Boyle a rest. While Boyle grazed on sweet grass, Murphy inspected Stuyvesant's tracks.

They weren't more than two days old. To reach the Rio Grande meant crossing some hard, dusty country that could wear out a horse, especially a wagon horse that wasn't used to carrying a rider and supplies across long distances.

Murphy looked at Boyle.

"We have a good chance of catching him," he said.

Burke stood before President Arthur's desk and held a very lengthy telegram in his right hand.

"Murphy trailed Stuyvesant to a general store in Arapahoe County owned by the Bensens," Burke said. "Reeva Bensen is the sister of John Quad."

"The mass killer from a few years ago?" Arthur said.

Burke nodded. "Before Garfield's assassination," he said. "Apparently Stuyvesant rode south after he shot Knoop, and Murphy picked up his trail. Stuyvesant rode into the general store, picked up supplies, and rode out. A week later, Murphy arrived, picked up supplies, and continued tracking Stuyvesant."

"To where?"

"South is all I can tell you," Burke said.

Arthur sighed loudly. "He could be in New Mexico or Arizona Territory by now, for all we know," he said.

"Sooner or later, he'll have to telegraph," Burke said.

"When he does, make no mention of his adopted baby," Arthur said. "We don't want to distract him from his task at hand."

Burke looked at Arthur.

"Do we, Mr. Burke?" Arthur said.

Murphy reached the fringe of the desert in northern New Mexico Territory shortly before sunset. He dismounted, checked Stuyvesant's tracks, and then made camp.

He built a fire and cooked bacon and beans in a pan, made a pot of coffee, and groomed Boyle.

"We have about thirty miles before we reach the Grande tomorrow, boy," Murphy said.

Boyle snorted as Murphy ran a brush against his back.

"I hope he doesn't get smart with us and try to backtrack to lose us," Murphy said.

Boyle snorted again.

"I know. You want your supper," Murphy said.

He filled the feedbag with a pound of grain. While Boyle ate, Murphy fixed a plate of bacon, beans, and cornbread for himself.

"Where is he going?" Murphy said. "Across the Grande to where?"

Murphy dug out his maps and studied them as he ate.

"If he's crossing the Grande, at this time of year it could be fifty feet deep and five hundred feet across," he said aloud. "He'll look for a river crossing."

Murphy looked at Boyle.

"And so will we," he said.

CHAPTER THIRTY-FOUR

Kai and Aideen shucked corn and beans on the porch while Knoop fed a bottle to the baby. Around the side of the house, Michael chopped wood.

"I'm going to town tomorrow to see if I have a telegram from my husband," Kai said.

"I'll go with you," Knoop said.

Aideen looked at Kai. "When my son joined the army and went off to war, I spent the first two years waiting for letters that never came. One, maybe two, a year to let me know he was alive. I would ride to his farm and check with his wife, but she never received letters either."

"I imagine with the war, there wasn't time to write," Kai said.

"It's more than that," Aideen said. "It's a self-defense technique. In order to survive, he needs to put thoughts of home out of his mind. As a lawman, he needs to do the same thing, because if he thinks of home too much, he'll get careless and then he won't come home at all."

Kai nodded. "I understand, but it's still difficult to just sit and wait."

"It's never easy, but at least you have a little something to occupy your time," Aideen said.

"The little something just wet her diaper and my pants," Knoop said.

★ ★ ★ ★ ★

As he crossed the northern tip of the desert, Murphy estimated the temperature to be at around ninety-five degrees.

It wasn't yet noon, but he had to dismount every few miles to try to pick up Stuyvesant's tracks. Desert winds made tracking very difficult. For a while, he thought he'd lost them entirely.

Around two in the afternoon, Murphy found a campsite. Some hard tracks that belonged to Stuyvesant's horse were visible.

He gave Boyle a one-hour rest.

"No water until it gets dark, or we reach the gorge and find water," Murphy said.

He checked the maps. They were close. He could see hills only about ten miles in the distance.

After that lay the gorge and the Rio Grande. After that, Santa Fe was a day's ride away.

The question was: on the other side of the Rio Grande, would Stuyvesant stop at Santa Fe, and if so, why? Or would he change direction and continue onward?

Murphy took stock of his supplies. He would need to resupply in Santa Fe if he was to keep pursuing Stuyvesant. For Stuyvesant to continue traveling, he would also need to resupply.

After the Grande, Santa Fe was the closest and largest town in which to do so.

Murphy mounted the saddle and gently tugged the reins.

"We'll find water in the gorge and camp for the night," he said to Boyle.

Murphy dismounted at a tributary stream of the Rio Grande and made camp. He built a fire and used a portable fishing line, using bread for bait, and snared two fish large enough for supper.

As he brushed Boyle, he kept an eye on the fish in the fry pan.

"In a while, when you've cooled down enough, I'll let you drink your fill," Murphy said.

The fish was a welcome change from beans and bacon. After eating, Boyle was cooled down enough that Murphy led him to the stream to drink.

While Boyle drank, Murphy stripped down, grabbed a bar of soap from the saddlebags, and waded into the cold water. After soaping up, Murphy dunked under the water and floated for a while.

Then he dried beside the fire and fed Boyle a pound of grain.

"Sometime tomorrow afternoon, we'll reach the Grande," he said to Boyle.

As he dressed, Murphy said, "We'll send Kai a wire and let Burke know where we are."

Boyle turned and looked at Murphy.

"I know, I want to go home too," Murphy said. "But we have to finish this first."

Traveling through the gorge was much cooler, and Boyle scarcely worked up a sweat. The air was saturated with water from the Rio Grande, only a few miles away. That also helped to keep Boyle's coat cool.

Around noon, Murphy rested Boyle for an hour. Murphy nibbled on cornbread with water while Boyle munched on grass.

After traveling for another hour, they reached the banks of the Rio Grande River. It was five hundred feet or more across and at least fifty feet deep.

"We'll need to find a crossing," Murphy said.

He checked his maps and found a crossing three miles to their south.

They'd ridden just a few minutes when Murphy spotted a

large raft tethered by thick ropes that spanned the width of the river.

A large cabin sat back from the banks. A handmade sign beside the raft read *River crossing one dollar per person. Fifty cents extra from the other side. Fifty cents extra for your horse.*

Another handmade sign was attached to the roof of the cabin that read *Ma's river crossing. No refunds.*

A heavyset woman in her sixties sat in a rocking chair on the porch and smoked a corncob pipe.

Four men sat in chairs beside her.

Murphy dismounted at the porch. "You must be Ma," he said.

"I am, and these are my sons," Ma said.

"I need to cross the river," Murphy said.

"Sit awhile, whoever you be, and have coffee with me," Ma said. "We don't cross a single rider. Our usual fare is four persons or more."

"I don't have time to wait, Ma," Murphy said. "I'll pay you twenty dollars to take me across right now."

"Are you a lawman of some kind? I don't see a badge," Ma said.

Murphy removed his wallet and held it up for Ma to see. "Federal. US Secret Service," he said.

"You have the look," Ma said. She turned to her four sons. "Ready the raft for crossing."

The four men stood and walked down from the porch.

"Come up and have coffee with me, federal lawman, while my boys ready the raft," Ma said.

Murphy went up and sat beside Ma. She lifted a large coffee pot off a table and filled a cup for him.

Murphy lit his pipe. "Can you help me with something else, Ma? I'll throw in ten dollars extra."

"You'll be after somebody, aren't you, lawman?" Ma said.

Murphy removed the folded photo of Stuyvesant from his shirt pocket and showed it to Ma.

"Yesterday noon, he crossed with five others," Ma said.

Murphy put the photo away and removed three ten-dollar gold pieces from his pants pocket and gave them to Ma.

One of Ma's sons approached the porch. "Raft is ready, Ma," he said.

Murphy stood. "Thanks for the coffee, Ma."

"Safe travels, lawman," Ma said.

Murphy and Boyle stood on the right side of the raft near its center, while the four brothers pulled the rope on the right side across five hundred feet of river. The rapids were strong, and the trip took nearly ten minutes. Exhausted, the four brothers finally docked the raft at the landing site on the opposite side of the Rio Grande.

"You boys rest up now," Murphy said as he gave each brother a five-dollar tip.

Murphy mounted the saddle and rode east toward Santa Fe. With a little luck, he would be halfway there by sunset.

Late in the afternoon, as he rode through rolling hills, Murphy heard gunshots echoing about a mile ahead.

He estimated at least a dozen different rifles and pistols were firing. He rode cautiously to a long bank of foothills where a dozen or more men were posted at various locations on the hills.

Each man had a rifle.

One man wearing a sheriff's badge shouted orders. "That's enough," he shouted. "All you're doing is making noise and wasting lead."

Murphy rode up behind the men and dismounted near the sheriff.

"Who are you?" the sheriff said.

247

"Murphy, US Secret Service," Murphy said and held up his identification.

"Langston, sheriff of Santa Fe. Is the president coming?" Langston said.

"No," Murphy said. "What's going on here?"

"Six assholes robbed the bank southeast of Santa Fe in the town of Las Vegas," Langston said. "We got them trapped down there in a gorge, but they won't go quietly."

Murphy glanced at the sun.

"Come dark, they'll slip out the back door," he said. "Send some men up behind them and close it."

"They have three rifles aimed our way and three to the rear," Langston said. "They already shot two of my posse, as it is."

Murphy nodded. "Well, good luck. I have pressing business."

"Now you hold your horses a second," Langston said. "Are you a lawman or not?"

"I'm federal," Murphy said.

"Robbing a bank is a federal crime, isn't it?" Langston said. "They killed a teller and the bank manager. That makes it your jurisdiction, doesn't it?"

Murphy sighed. "Let me take a look."

Murphy and Langston went to the edge of the hill, got on their stomachs, and gazed down into a shallow gorge.

"Behind those big rocks," Langston said.

"After dark they can walk their horses in either direction without being seen," Murphy said.

"That's why we're trying to keep them pinned down," Langston said.

"It will be dark in an hour," Murphy said.

"I know that, but what am I supposed to do? Ride down into six rifles waiting to pick us off," Langston said.

Murphy stood up. "Call in your men. I have an idea."

Langston called in the posse of twelve men.

"Every man, gather up as much tumbleweed as possible," Murphy said. "If anybody has liquor, wet it just after dark. When you hear movement, light the tumbleweed and toss it over the side to the west to block their path. I'll be on the east."

"What do you mean you'll be on the east?" Langston said.

"In the gorge," Murphy said. "You men go, gather up tumbleweed, and make sure it's as dry as possible."

"I should go with you," Langston said.

"You'll only be in my way," Murphy said. "After dark, when you hear horses start to move, have your men light the tumbleweeds and throw them into the west side of the gorge about a hundred yards from here."

"All right," Langston said. "But I really should go with you."

"I'm better alone," Murphy said.

Murphy went to Boyle and removed his extra Colt revolver from a saddlebag. He checked to ensure it was loaded and placed it inside his gun belt.

"Don't touch my horse," Murphy told Langston. "He doesn't take to strangers."

Murphy walked three hundred feet to the east and waited for the sun to sink below the horizon of the hills. Then he slid down the side of the hill to the bottom of the gorge, got behind a large rock, and waited.

Once the sun was past the horizon, the gorge was totally dark. Murphy could hear movement ahead, made by both men and horses.

Murphy looked up and watched as dozens of flaming tumbleweeds soared down the side of the hill.

"It's a trap," one of the bank robbers yelled.

Murphy stood up and walked west inside the gorge. The light of the burning tumbleweeds illuminated his way. When six riders came charging directly at him, he drew both Colts, cocked them, and waited until they were in range.

Murphy fired one shot in the air and the six riders stopped their horses.

The riders couldn't see Murphy, but he could see them as the light from the tumbleweed fires was at their backs.

"Surrender right now, or I will kill you where you stand," Murphy said.

"Surrender to who?" a rider called out.

"Murphy, federal officer," Murphy said.

"Well, Murphy, federal officer, you can screw yourself from here to Sunday," a rider said.

Murphy sighed. He was a faster draw with his right hand than the left, but he was equally good a shot with either hand.

He cocked both Colts, fired them both, and two men fell from their horses. One man crawled on the ground but stopped moving when Murphy shot him a second time.

"In case you were wondering, I wasn't asking. Who wants to be next?" Murphy said.

"Hold on, just you hold on," a rider said.

"Toss your guns—rifles, too—and get down off your horses," Murphy said.

Revolvers and rifles hit the ground.

"Left to right, step down from your horse and get on the ground," Murphy said.

One at a time, the riders dismounted and lay on their stomachs.

"Sheriff Langston, have your men come down and take these men into custody," Murphy called.

Around a large campfire, Murphy, Langston, the posse, and the tied-up outlaws ate plates of hot beef stew.

"Well, Mr. Federal Lawman, you certainly have balls of cast iron," Langston said.

"What I have is the experience to deal with simpletons like

those men," Murphy said.

"I don't care how much experience you have, it took a lot of hard bark to walk down there like that," Langston said.

Murphy took a sip of coffee from a tin cup. "How far to Santa Fe?"

"Forty miles," Langston said. "I never did ask. What's your business in Santa Fe?"

"Do you read the newspapers much?" Murphy said.

CHAPTER THIRTY-FIVE

Burke stood before President Arthur's desk while Arthur read a report from a US marshal in Oklahoma.

Arthur sighed. "The wife of a man on trial for murder shot a jury member in the street, and the judge declared a mistrial because no one will now sit on a jury panel," he said.

"The woman was arrested for the murder of the jury member," Burke said.

"It's not good enough to stop this madness," Arthur said. "We need Murphy to bring Stuyvesant in alive, so he can be tried and hanged in the public square with great fanfare."

Burke nodded. "I'll check to see if Murphy has telegraphed," he said.

Kai held the baby while she waited on the porch with Aideen and Knoop for Michael to bring the wagon around from the barn.

"You and Michael don't have to stay, you know," Kai said. "I really am fine, and Melvin will stay until Murphy returns."

"Do you really think you can convince Michael to leave at this point?" Aideen said.

"No, I suppose not," Kai said.

"Like father, like son," Aideen said.

Murphy and Langston rode ahead of the posse and reached Santa Fe by three in the afternoon.

It was a large town of nearly seven thousand residents, first settled more than a hundred years ago along the banks of the Santa Fe River.

Murphy was familiar with the town, having stayed there several times in the past.

The two men dismounted at Langston's office

"How many general stores are there in town?" Murphy said.

"Four."

"If Stuyvesant rode in, it was to get supplies. We'll try those places first," Murphy said.

After leaving the fourth general store without results, Murphy said, "How many livery stables?"

"Three."

The manager of the third livery stable, after viewing the photo of Stuyvesant, said, "Yesterday morning, he sold me his horse and rig for one hundred and fifty dollars. Said he wouldn't need them anymore."

"Is the horse still here?" Murphy said.

"Stall number nine," the manager said.

Murphy and Langston went to stall nine, and Murphy checked the horse's right front shoe. "This is the horse Stuyvesant rode after he butchered a Mormon family when his own horse went lame," he said.

Murphy and Langston returned to the manager.

"Did he buy another horse?" Murphy said.

"He did not," the manager said. "Not here, anyway."

Outside the stable, Murphy said, "Let's check the hotels."

The desk clerk at the Hotel Santa Fe looked at Stuyvesant's photograph and said, "He didn't look like that when he checked in."

"What do you mean?" Murphy said.

"He was rough around the edges, if you know what I mean," the clerk said. "Scraggly beard and hair, tattered clothes. The first thing he did was order a bath and a shave. When he checked out this morning, he was wearing a new suit of clothes and looked like he does in that photograph."

"Did he say where he was going?" Murphy said.

"No, and I didn't ask," the clerk said.

Murphy looked at Langston. "Let's check the railroad."

From behind his desk the station manager said, "I have no idea if this man took a train at any time today. Check with my clerks at the counter."

"Call them in here," Murphy said.

The station manager stared at Murphy.

"That wasn't a request," Murphy said.

The station manager stood from behind his desk, went to the door, opened it, and went outside. He returned a minute later with the two ticket clerks.

Murphy showed them Stuyvesant's photograph. "Did this man buy a ticket here today?" he said.

One of the clerks nodded. "He bought a one-way ticket to New York City on the noon train," he said.

Murphy looked at the large clock on the wall. "Six hours ago," he said.

"It ran about fifteen minutes late," the clerk said.

"How many people are on that train?" Murphy said.

"A hundred and fifty at least," the clerk said.

Murphy looked at the station manager. "If a train with just three cars left here and ran at full speed, where could it overtake the New York–bound train?"

"Why, that's crazy," the station manager said.

"Maybe so, but that's what we're going to do," Murphy said.

"I can't just . . . the railroad is federally controlled," the station manager said. "It would take the board of directors to—"

"I'll get a directive directly from the president," Murphy said.

"Get a train ready with three cars, and have it standing by. Figure out the route and time. I'll be right back."

Burke showed Murphy's telegram to President Arthur, who read it behind his desk in the Oval Office.

"I could contact the railroad and stop the train," Arthur said.

"And risk the lives of a hundred and fifty passengers on board?" Burke said. "Think of the negative press you would have to explain, come election time. Murphy knows what he's doing; we should let him do it."

Arthur sighed. "Why New York City? He could have hidden out for years undetected."

"To finish what he started?" Burke said.

"Do it," Arthur said.

Burke nodded, turned, and left the Oval Office.

The Santa Fe Railroad Station had its own telegraph in a back room. Murphy copied the response he'd received from Burke and showed it to Langston.

Langston read the reply and said, "That station manager is going to want to keep this and hang it over his desk."

"I'll frame it for him if he gets me a train," Murphy said.

The station manager was at a large table in his office where he was studying a map of railroad routes, when Murphy and Langston entered. Murphy handed the station manager the telegraph from President Arthur.

"Sheriff Langston, ask one of my clerks to come in here," the station manager said.

Langston went out for a moment.

Murphy looked at the maps on the table. "Have you worked it out?"

"Not yet. Almost."

Langston returned with a ticket clerk.

"Get the yardmaster, Kingston, in here right away," the station manager said. "And all engineers standing by."

Murphy, Kingston, and three engineers stood around the table and looked at the map, as the station manager traced a path with a pencil.

"The noon to New York has a one-hour layover in Dodge City, another one-hour layover in Topeka, and another in Kansas City. In between, they have a dozen water stops," the station manager said. "The noon to New York is hauling a dozen cars, a hundred and fifty passengers, plus a boxcar, and will be traveling at an average speed of forty miles an hour. If you leave now, carrying just a riding car and boxcar and travel full throttle, you could reach Kansas City about thirty minutes before them."

"On the freight tracks?" an engineer said.

"Yes, exactly," the station manager said. "Skirt the big towns by using the freight tracks."

"You'll have to clear it," the engineer said.

"It's already been cleared," the station manager said and nodded to Murphy. "By him."

"How long to reach Kansas City?" Murphy said.

"Six hundred miles at fifty-five, sometimes sixty miles an hour, add in water stops, and I'd say twelve hours," the station manager said.

"I'll get my horse and meet you in the yard in fifteen minutes," Murphy said.

After loading Boyle into the boxcar, Murphy met Langston and the station manager on the dark platform. The station manager carried an oil lantern.

"Good luck to you, and thanks for your help with the bank robbers," Langston said.

"It's been an interesting day," the station manager said. "It has been that," Murphy said and boarded the train.

"It's been an interesting day," the station manager said. "It has been that," Murphy said and boarded the train.

CHAPTER THIRTY-SIX

The only available riding car was actually a dining car. Shortly after the train left Santa Fe, Murphy made a pot of coffee.

Two of the engineers were in the engine car, while the third shared a table with Murphy and drank coffee.

"This man you're after must be one bad *hombre*," the engineer said.

Murphy lit his pipe and nodded. "He's murdered at least fourteen people in cold blood that I'm aware of," he said.

"How do you murder fourteen people in cold blood?" the engineer said.

"Start by being insane and don't have a conscience," Murphy said.

The engineer nodded and sipped his coffee.

At the first water stop, the engineers rotated their duties. The dining car was stocked with canned goods, and Murphy prepared a large cauldron of beef stew. An engineer ate a bowl of stew with Murphy, then the engineer took two bowls to the engine car.

Alone at a table, Murphy sipped coffee, smoked his pipe, and field-stripped and cleaned his Colt revolver. When it was spotless, he polished each bullet with a napkin and then reloaded the Colt.

At the second water stop, Murphy went to the engine car to shovel coal. He removed his shirt and holster and got to work.

For two hours he sweated, shoveling coal into the furnace.

After the third water stop, Murphy returned to the dining car and grabbed some sleep on the floor. When he awoke, the sun was shining in through the windows and the engineer was drinking coffee at a table.

Murphy stood up, filled a cup with coffee, and took a seat at the table with the engineer.

"We'll be in Kansas City in two hours," the engineer said.

Murphy sipped coffee and nodded.

"This outlaw on the train, he's that 'Ghost Shooter' from the newspapers, isn't he?" the engineer said.

"He is," Murphy said.

"And it's just you?"

"He's shown he's not afraid to kill innocent strangers," Murphy said. "If he suspects he's being followed, he has a hundred and fifty–plus targets readily at hand."

The engineer nodded. "I think I'll fix some eggs. Do you want some eggs?"

Burke stood before President Arthur's desk shortly before seven in the morning.

"What time is the noon train from Santa Fe scheduled to arrive in Kansas City?" Arthur said.

"In about an hour," Burke said.

"I suppose it's too late to mobilize the army or a team of marshals to Kansas City," Arthur said.

"I think doing that would only get innocent passengers killed," Burke said.

Arthur nodded. "Get down to the telegraph room and wait for Murphy to contact us," he said.

Burke turned and walked to the door.

"And William, tell my staff to bring me some breakfast," Arthur said.

Murphy rode with the engineer in the engine car as the train slowly rolled to a stop in the stockyards of Kansas City, Kansas. The engineer could see across the yards to the station where the noon train from Santa Fe was stopped at the platform.

"Looks like they beat us here, but not by much," the engineer said.

"Stay put and make sure nobody goes near my horse," Murphy said. "He doesn't take to strangers."

Murphy jumped to the ground and walked from the stockyards to the depot, where the passenger train was in the station.

A conductor stood at the first riding car.

Murphy removed his wallet and showed the conductor his identification.

"Is the president here?" the conductor said.

"No. Get up with the engineer. This train doesn't move until I say it moves," Murphy said.

The conductor looked at Murphy.

"I wasn't asking," Murphy said.

The conductor went to the engine car and climbed aboard.

Murphy entered the first riding car, where five passengers had remained seated during the layover.

They looked at him as he walked through the car, opened the sliding door, and entered the second car.

One woman sat beside a window with a sleeping baby in her arms.

Murphy moved to the third car, which was empty.

Three men occupied the fourth car, none of whom was Stuyvesant.

The fifth and sixth cars were empty.

The seventh and eighth cars were sleeping cars. A porter was on duty in the hallway.

Murphy showed the porter his identification and Stuyvesant's photograph.

"Have you seen this man aboard this train?" Murphy said.

The porter nodded. "Berth number eleven, but he left the train about fifteen minutes ago," he said.

"Are you sure?" Murphy said.

"Yes, sir. He was wearing a new suit of clothes and a gentleman's hat," the porter said.

"Stay on the train," Murphy said.

Murphy left the sleeper car, stood beside the train, and watched as dozens of passengers returned from town.

Murphy kept still and scanned the crowd as it approached the train.

About forty feet away, he spotted Stuyvesant. Dressed in a new suit of clothes, a fine Bowler hat on his head, he was smoking a cigar and carrying a newspaper.

When Stuyvesant was twenty feet from Murphy, he looked at Murphy and paused. Instinctively, Stuyvesant knew Murphy was here for him.

The newspaper fell from his hand and he reached inside his suit jacket for his .36 caliber Colt revolver.

Stuyvesant cocked the revolver, aimed, and fired at Murphy.

Murphy didn't move as the ball went wide and struck a portly woman in the leg as she was attempting to board the train. The woman screamed.

Murphy drew his Colt and waited.

At the sound of Stuyvesant's shot, the crowd got down or fled, but Stuyvesant grabbed a woman and held her by the neck.

"I will kill this woman," Stuyvesant said. "You know I will, so back off."

"If you kill that woman, I will kill you," Murphy said.

"I'm going to New York to claim my son," Stuyvesant said.

"I'm afraid not," Murphy said. "You're coming with me to stand trial for the innocent people you murdered."

"Innocent!" Stuyvesant shouted. His grip on the woman's neck tightened. "They sent me to prison for a dozen years for doing what any man would have done to a cheating wife. I was off to war, and she was taking another man into our bed. A bed I paid for. Don't tell me they're innocent, because they're not. I was innocent, and they sent me away for a dozen years. Now, if you don't mind, my son is waiting for me back home."

Murphy looked into Stuyvesant's eyes. Knoop was right, the man was insane and too far gone to reason with.

Stuyvesant placed the .36 caliber Colt against the woman's head. She closed her eyes tight.

"Now, let me leave or this woman dies," Stuyvesant said.

Murphy drew a shallow breath as he cocked his Colt.

His own words echoed through his mind.

A Regulator is a killer of men.

A killer of men.

Maybe.

But not today.

Murphy brought his Colt up to eye level.

He fired, and the shot struck Stuyvesant in his right hand. The .36 Colt revolver fell from his grasp as the bullet tore through the flesh of his hand and pierced his upper right chest.

The woman broke free and ran toward Murphy.

Murphy walked to Stuyvesant.

"They'll hang me," Stuyvesant said.

"Yes, they will," Murphy said and flipped his Colt around and smacked Stuyvesant across the face with the heavy butt, knocking the man unconscious to the platform.

Burke brought President Arthur Murphy's telegram the moment he received it.

"That son of a bitch pulled it off," Arthur said. "Have a telegram sent to every major newspaper in the country, and then schedule a press conference on the lawn right after lunch."

Burke nodded and turned to the door.

"And get down to Fort Smith right away," Arthur said. "I want you to hold a press conference on the steps of the courthouse. Make sure every reporter understands that the government, local and federal, won't tolerate terrorism in any form. Our country runs on the rule of law, and our judicial system must never be compromised."

Burke reached for the doorknob.

"By this time tomorrow, the stock market will be up three hundred points," Arthur said.

"I'm sure it will be," Burke said.

"We've avoided a major recession like the one in seventy-three," Arthur said.

"Apparently so, sir," Burke said.

"And make sure Murphy doesn't run for public office ever again," Arthur said.

Burke looked back at Arthur.

"He's far too valuable to waste on public service," Arthur said.

Burke sighed, nodded, and opened the door.

Chapter Thirty-Seven

Judge Parker and William Burke stood front and center on the platform as they waited for Murphy's train to arrive.

US Marshals Cal Witson and Bass Reeves stood directly behind them.

Behind Witson and Reeves, Kai held the baby. Next to Kai stood Aideen, Michael, and Knoop.

Otherwise, the station was closed and void of passengers.

"I do believe I see the train coming," Parker said.

Murphy sat at the table in the dining car, smoked his pipe, sipped coffee, and watched Stuyvesant, who sat across from him.

Stuyvesant was in leg irons and handcuffs.

"Why did you bother to have the doctor remove the bullet from my chest? It would have been simpler to just let me die," Stuyvesant said.

"It's called the rule of law," Murphy said. "You will receive a fair trial and be represented by the best attorney possible."

"And then hanged," Stuyvesant said.

"That's not for me to say," Murphy said.

"They took my life, your rule of law," Stuyvesant said. "My wife, she ran around with another man while I was off defending my country. You call that fair? You call that just?"

"You talk like you're the only man who ever lost something in that damned war," Murphy said. "I lost my wife and family, and more than a half million people lost their lives. So your wife cheated on you, so what? That doesn't give you the right to murder people in cold blood."

"And what gives you the right to hang me?" Stuyvesant said.

"A jury," Murphy said.

Murphy led Stuyvesant off the train where Witson and Reeves took him into custody and whisked him away.

"On behalf of the President of the United States, I would like to—" Burke said.

Kai stepped between Parker and Burke with the baby in her arms.

"Forget all that mumbo jumbo," she said. "Murphy, meet your daughter."

ABOUT THE AUTHOR

Ethan J. Wolfe is the author of a dozen western novels, including the highly praised Regulator historical novels.

The employees of Five Star Publishing hope you have enjoyed this book.

Our Five Star novels explore little-known chapters from America's history, stories told from unique perspectives that will entertain a broad range of readers.

Other Five Star books are available at your local library, bookstore, all major book distributors, and directly from Five Star/Gale.

Connect with Five Star Publishing

Visit us on Facebook:
https://www.facebook.com/FiveStarCengage

Email:
FiveStar@cengage.com

For information about titles and placing orders:
(800) 223-1244
gale.orders@cengage.com

To share your comments, write to us:
Five Star Publishing
Attn: Publisher
10 Water St., Suite 310
Waterville, ME 04901